**Madison wanted Sam as much as he did her. But fear had her fighting her desire all the way. Something he understood completely.**

But… One kiss. What harm could that do? It wouldn't mean there was more to come, but it would satisfy an ache.

Or create a bigger one.

There was that.

One kiss would definitely crank up the heat into an inferno.

But he had to taste her. Had to know those lips—had to satisfy a quest he'd begun unknowingly only days ago. At the same time it was as though all the barriers he'd erected were tightening, warning him, *Don't do it*. But the clawing need for affection and sharing was stronger.

'I think I'll head inside.' Madison stood before him, looking sad and lost.

Sam did what he shouldn't. He ignored those damned warnings.

Dear Reader,

Almost everyone has scars—mental and/or physical. Some are minor, others serious, but all affect the person carrying them. These scars and how they're coped with are what make people interesting.

In *Resisting Her Army Doc Rival* Captain Madison Hunter has had more than her share of bad luck, which has left her unable to show anyone her body and thus keeps her away from getting close to men. Captain Sam Lowe isn't bothered by that— he's got his own guilt to deal with, and he finds Maddy fascinating and beautiful. But she's no longer the bright, bubbly personality he vaguely remembers from school. And the sadness lurking in her eyes and her fear of smoke has him pulling up the barriers around his soul so fast it's bewildering. But there's something about this woman he can't ignore. If he was ever to put his heart on the line and get close to someone it would be Maddy who'd make him do it.

This story didn't come easily for me. There's a lot of pain in my hero and my heroine, and I really wanted them to have their moment—to learn to live freely again and know what it's like not to be on guard all the time. But they didn't make it simple for me. Oh, no. Every word and emotion was dragged out onto the page, and I'm relieved they finally got their happy ending.

I hope you root for these two as you read their story.

Drop by and let me know if they affected you as they did me: sue.mackay56@yahoo.com. Or visit my website: suemackay.co.nz.

Cheers,

*Sue MacKay*

# RESISTING HER ARMY DOC RIVAL

## BY
## SUE MacKAY

WARWICKSHIRE
COUNTY LIBRARY

CONTROL No.

MILLS
BOON

First published in Great Britain 2017
By Mills & Boon, an imprint of HarperCollins*Publishers*
1 London Bridge Street, London, SE1 9GF

Large Print edition 2017

© 2017 Sue MacKay

ISBN: 978-0-263-06723-1

Printed and bound in Great Britain
by CPI Antony Rowe, Chippenham, Wiltshire

**Sue MacKay** lives with her husband in New Zealand's beautiful Marlborough Sounds, with the water at her doorstep and the birds and the trees at her back door. It is the perfect setting to indulge her passions of entertaining friends by cooking them sumptuous meals, drinking fabulous wine, going for hill walks or kayaking around the bay—and, of course, writing stories.

## Books by Sue MacKay

### Mills & Boon Medical Romance

*Midwife...to Mum!*
*Reunited...in Paris!*
*A December to Remember*
*Breaking All Their Rules*
*Dr White's Baby Wish*
*The Army Doc's Baby Bombshell*

Visit the Author Profile page
at millsandboon.co.uk for more titles.

To the most gorgeous and precious
wee people in my life. Grandies Austin and
Taylor. I love you to bits and can't believe
how lucky I am to get Austin hugs
and Taylor smiles.

And to Laura McCallen for your unfailing
patience to see me through this story. (At
least you appeared patient from my end.) :)

**Praise for
Sue MacKay**

'I highly recommend this story to all lovers
of romance: it is moving, emotional, a joy
o read!'

—*Goodreads* on
*A December to Remember*

# CHAPTER ONE

CAPTAIN MADISON HUNTER stepped out of the New Zealand Air Force freight plane and onto the tarmac, relieved to be on terra firma at last, flying being her least favourite of the things she had to do. Then the searing heat of the Sinai Peninsula slammed into her, ramping up the discomfort level and making her gasp.

'Who needs this?'

'Beats Waiouru in winter any day,' quipped the communications major striding alongside her. His energy was embarrassing after all those hours crammed between cargo crates, doing nothing more intelligent than playing endless rounds of poker.

'Guess that's because you've been here before. Right now I'd be happy marching through snow and sleet,' Madison retorted, thinking longingly of the isolated army base where she'd done her basic training, hell hole of the North Island that it was.

'At least your boots will be dry.'

'True.' Sodden boots were the bane of army exercises back home. They never dried out before the next foray. Looking at the dusty ground in front of her, she finally smiled. 'This couldn't be more different. Exciting even.' If she could ignore the heat.

Heaving the thirty-kilogram pack higher on her back, Madison rolled her shoulders to ease the tightness. Didn't work. Sweat streamed over her shoulder blades, down her face, between her breasts. *Must have been out of my mind when I signed up.* 'Did I miss the clause in my contract saying beware of sun, sand, dirt, and sweat enough to drown a small creature?'

'Page three,' quipped Major Crooks.

'I take it the high temperature is relentless.' Dry heat shimmered against the white block buildings, while the air was almost cracking. Off-duty soldiers lounged in what little shade they could find.

'I never got used to it on my last tour.' He

pointed across the dusty parade ground. 'See that building to the right? It's the medical unit.'

Madison scoped the basic structure with a faded red cross painted above the door. Less than what she'd worked in on base at home, more than she'd been led to believe she'd find here. Had to be a positive. 'I might drop in after a shower.' If she didn't fall asleep standing under the water. Her body ached with fatigue. There hadn't been a lot of sleeping going on during the flight. She probably stank like a piece of roadkill about now.

A man stepped through the medical unit's entrance, and paused. Tall and broad shouldered, his body tapered down to the narrow hips his hands settled on. Looking in their direction, his gaze finally settled on her.

Sam Lowe? As in the guy every girl from high school had fallen in love with Sam Lowe?

Her knees sagged, and not from the load on her back.

Seriously? Someone she knew from home when home had been Christchurch? Now, there was a surprise that lightened her mood a notch. Not that they'd been friends in any way but she'd grab at any familiar face in an alien environment; until she'd settled in, any rate. Unless she'd got it wrong, and that wasn't Sam.

'Are you all right?' Major Crooks asked.

'Fine. Where're our barracks, do you know?'

He pointed. 'Over to the right, behind the mess block are the officers' quarters.'

'Thanks, I'll catch up with you later.' Right now Madison wanted to check out the man she thought she recognised, but was probably so far off the mark she'd sound stupid uttering his name.

She squinted through the heat. No doubting the vision that reminded her of standing on the side of the rugby field, barracking for their high school team as he led them to yet another win. It was definitely Sam Lowe striding towards her, those long legs eating up the ground like nothing bothered him. It probably didn't. Those shoulders and the cocky tip of his head backed up what her eyes were seeing, but there was little else she knew about him, she realised.

'Captain Hunter, Madison.' The man had the nerve to snap to attention in front of her. And grin. *He still does that.* Smiled and grinned his way into and out of every situation he faced. An expert, no less, she now recalled. *Still arrogant?* Well, she wasn't a spoilt brat any more—if she'd ever been—so possibly he'd changed, too.

'Sam,' she replied, at a loss for words. She didn't trust unexpected surprises. They tended to backfire on her.

He said, 'Welcome to the Sinai.'

Her voice returned, spilling out more than was necessary. 'I can't believe this. We're both in the army, posted to the same region, on the same base?' What were the odds? They even had rank in common. Her teeth ground back and forth. Slim to zilch. Showed how wrong she got things these days, despite the harsh lessons she'd endured already. A medical insignia told her more. 'You're a doctor, too.'

He nodded. 'We've been expecting you.'

'As in me personally?' Of course her name would've been on the staff list that'd have come through days ago. But, 'I doubt you realised who I was,' she retorted, suddenly on edge in front of that dazzling smile, and needing to shield herself from its dangerous intensity. So? Relax. She knew how to cope with men, had learned the hard way to always be careful and cautious. Just ignore them. Easy-peasy.

'As in a new medic, fresh from home and not worn down by the day-to-day grind of living in camp.' He widened his grin. 'And, yes, as in Madison Hunter, high school prefect and science genius.'

Oh, yeah, it would be too easy to fall into that grin, and forget the pain of being betrayed after trusting a man with her heart once already. Reining in the bewilderment overtaking her faster than a speeding bullet, she stood to attention. 'So we'll be working together?'

'I'll be out of your hair next week.'

He wasn't getting anywhere near her hair. But was he admiring it? Yeah, he was. Something like shock diluted that brazen glare he'd been delivering.

Fair cop. She did look very different these days. Her waist-length hair had fallen prey to the hairdresser's scissors the day after she'd joined the army. Crawling under barbed wire through mud and snow while dressed in full army kit had made the thick locks she'd considered her best feature very unattractive and in need of constant attention. What had Sam been talking about? Apart from hair? 'So you're one of the medics I'm replacing.'

'Afraid so.' His shoulder moved, oh so nonchalantly.

That grin was now crooked. Instead of loosening the hold it held over her, she was drawn in deeper. It was beguiling and threatening in an I-can't-afford-to-check-this-out kind of way. Desperate for a distraction—no, Sam already had that role—Madison glanced around the compound. She checked out the perimeter fence and saw women, men and children sitting in a huddle, resignation on their faces.

'Why are there civilians waiting outside the camp?'

'They're hoping to see a doctor or nurse.'

Her heart tightened for the sad-looking bunch of people. They appeared helpless, lost even. It took all her willpower not to drop her pack and race across to ask what she could do for them.

That was one of the reasons she'd joined the army after all. 'I want to help them.'

'It's not that easy, Madison.'

'Why not?' She flung the words at him. 'It's why I became a doctor. Isn't it the same for you?'

He took her question on the chin. 'I understand, but out here you're a soldier first, doctor second.'

'So you're saying we ignore those people?' Her hand flapped through the air in the direction of the perimeter. 'Seriously?'

'No, I'm not.' Sam's mouth tightened as his gaze stopped on the people she'd noted. 'We do see some of the locals under a strict system involving body searches and metal detectors before bringing them in.'

'We don't hold regular clinics?' She'd been told she would be attending to outsiders, and had been keen to get amongst them.

'More than enough,' he grunted, 'but so many people require medical attention it'd be a never-ending stream if we allowed it.' Sam locked his now fierce eyes on her. 'We do our share. Remember why you're here, Captain.'

'But there are children out there.' She couldn't help wanting to help each and every person in that crowd waiting quietly as though they had nothing better to do, but especially the children. They were pulling at her heartstrings already. It would be a struggle not being allowed to put her medical skills to good use as she wanted when there were people needing them. That was why she'd trained in the first place, to make life better for others, especially children now that she likely wouldn't be having any herself.

'Yes, there are. Cute as buttons some of them, too.' His face softened briefly.

'They look so desperate.'

Sam shook himself and growled, 'Don't be fooled. They're not all what they seem.' He started walking again.

'They're not?' But he didn't, or chose not to, hear her.

On a sigh she changed the subject. For now. 'I'll see you around. I need to find my quarters.'

'I'll—'

'I don't think so. Major Crooks gave me directions.' Then she added lamely, just in case Sam didn't get the point, 'He's been here before.' Having this man escort her through the camp was not happening. She required a few minutes to put her left-field reaction to him into perspective. He might be a sight to behold, and a face from the past, but she had to learn to stand strong and inviolate. Vulnerability might've become her norm lately, but it was one of the things she was working hard to overcome. So when her danger sonar said be aware of this man, she was going to push him away.

'I was about to say I'll see you later in the medical unit, where I can introduce you to everyone.' He stared at her, annoyance vying with interest in those eyes that appeared to notice far too much, his mouth flat at last.

While *her* mouth ached with the tight smile she was trying to keep in place. Her eyes had better be fierce, not showing her true concerns about this exchange. Having anyone know her inner turmoil would see her back on that plane, heading home. 'Yes, Captain.'

His face instantly became inscrutable, every last thought and emotion snapped off with the flick of a switch. Her tense muscles tightened further. She'd gone too far. He didn't deserve her attitude, but a woman had to look out for herself. Especially in a place she did not understand. In a fit of pique for coming second to her in an exam result Sam had once told her she was a spoilt little rich brat, and right now she was proving him correct. He'd also said she knew nothing about the real world. *If only he knew.* Back up. She didn't want him to know about the disaster that flipped her life upside down.

Suddenly she was tired of it all; exhausted from the trip, from the heat, from the short but stupid conversation with Sam. She wanted to get on with him, maybe get to know him a little— without falling into that grin. 'I look forward to learning the ropes from you.'

'I'll see you later.' Sam's boots clicked together, then he spun around to stride away, his back ramrod straight, his hands clenched at his sides.

*He's better looking than ever.* Shut up. But it was true. The boyishly handsome and beguiling face had become chiselled, mature, and worthy of more than a glance. As was that muscular bod.

Her traitorous body was reacting to the thought of what his army fatigues covered. Only because there'd been a sex drought in her life for so long, surely? Not that Sam would be the rain that broke it, even if her body was thinking otherwise.

Heatstroke. Had to be. But she'd been out in the sun less than half an hour. Admitting things about a man she'd met minutes earlier would have more to do with her wobbly state of mind. Things that weren't conducive to working alongside him. Captain Lowe. Remember that and forget his looks, his muscles, and that open face she'd managed to shut down. But she was female after all and did enjoy being around a good-looking guy. She wasn't immune to physical attributes that would send any breathing, feeling woman into orbit. Despite the fact that letting down the barriers so that a man could get close would take more guts than she possessed, she could still appreciate perfection when she saw it.

Maddy shook her head abruptly. *You came here to do a job, not to fire up your hormones.* Experience had taught her that she couldn't do casual sex; she had to have some connection with a lover. When she'd fallen in love she'd known it had been worth the wait. Until that man, who had become her husband, had pulverised her heart along with her confidence, and she was back to square one. She was unlikely to ever forget Jason's appalled reaction to her disfigured body. She'd believed in his love. Now she knew not to expect any different from any man, so knew keeping safe was entirely up to herself.

'Captain? Your room is number three in that block behind the mess hall.' A soldier appeared in her line of vision, a clipboard in his hand, thankfully blotting out that irritating sight of long legs and tight backside that had her in a spin.

'Thank you, Private,' she acknowledged as she turned in the right direction.

One step and Madison froze.

Thick smoke billowed above a hut on the far perimeter.

A chill slithered down her spine, lifted the hairs on her arms. Her heart leapt into her throat. She forgot to breathe. 'No.' The word crawled out of her mouth as fear swamped her. 'No-o.' Smoke meant fire. No, please, no. She couldn't deal with that. Not today. Not ever. Not again. Anything else, yes. *Move. Run.* Someone could be trapped inside the hut. *Move.* She remained transfixed, staring at that murky column rising into the air, twisting, spiralling out of control.

'Move, damn it.' *Do something.* But her boots were filled with concrete. 'I can't.' Her fingers touched her midriff, not feeling the scars through her uniform, but they were there, as familiar to her touch as her face in a mirror was to her sight.

'Madison?' Sam stood in front of her.

She tried to look away from that smoke. She really did. But her eyes had a mind of their own, were fixated with the swirling, growing cloud. As the smoke darkened, horror darkened her soul. Knots cramped her stomach. Bile spewed into her mouth, soured her tongue. Finally her lungs moved, expanded slowly against her chest.

Strong hands caught her upper arms, shook her. 'Captain Hunter, what's the problem?'

The air stalled in her lungs again. *Breathe out slowly; one, two, three. Now in, one, two.* 'There's a fire.' She jerked her chin in the right direction as her lungs contracted, forcing hot air through her mouth.

Sam glanced where she'd indicated. 'That's not smoke. It's a dust whirl. Get used to it. We get plenty around here.' That intense stare returned to her face. What was he seeing? Apart from someone who should be behaving like a soldier? And clearly wasn't.

'You're sure? You haven't gone to check it out.'

'I'm sure.'

Her knees sagged, and her shoulders drooped further into his strong grip. Air escaped her lungs again. 'D-dust I can cope with.' Phew. She was safe; she didn't have to rush into roaring flames to rescue Granddad, pull him free of burning timbers. Except she hadn't managed to save him. A blazing beam had seen to that. The sweat on her back chilled, her damaged skin prickled. Granddad.

Someone was shaking her. Sam. Of course. 'Madison, look at me.'

*I can't do that.* He'd see right inside, would know she was a screw-up. Nothing like the confident girl who used to cope with everything and had always been a success. She certainly didn't used to do vulnerable. Digging deep, she tried to find that Madison, but she was long gone. Burned in the midst of a fire. 'I'm all right. I don't mind dust.' That scratchy sound coming across her tongue was not her usual voice; instead, it sounded like a cat when its tail was stomped on.

'You won't be saying that for long. It never goes away, coats every damned surface, and gets into places you won't believe.'

*But it won't kill me, or scar my body, or terrify me. Or take someone I love. Or change my life for ever.* Shaking in her boots, she continued staring at the thinning cloud as it changed direction to head away from the buildings. A grenade had been lobbed at her within minutes of arriving. This place was not good for her.

Just as well Sam still held her. To hit the ground with thirty kilos on her back would hurt, and write her off as a loser in everyone's eyes.

Did he know he was rubbing her arms with his thumbs? Couldn't, or he'd stop immediately. She didn't want that. Not yet. She needed the contact, the comfort, which showed how messed up she was. She was an officer in the New Zealand army, for pity's sake. 'It's truly only dust?'

'Yes, Madison, not smoke.'

The unexpected gentleness in his voice nearly undid her. She wasn't used to that tone from men any more, and it reached inside to tear at her heart, slashed at the barricades she kept wound tight. She tilted forward, drawn by an invisible thread, needing to get closer. Her brain was begging Sam to wrap his arms around her.

Her chin flipped up. Under pressure from her pack she straightened her spine and locked her eyes on his. He'd have her back on that plane heading home quick smart if he knew what she wanted of him. Good idea. That'd get her away from here and everything she suspected was going to test her over the coming weeks and months. Something at the back of her mind was pushing forward. *I am not a coward.* Not even a little one? *No. Not even a tiny one.* Messed up? *Yes.* But she would not add coward to her CV. Twisting her head away from that all-seeing gaze, she locked her eyes on the dust that had ripped her equilibrium apart.

'Dust can be a nuisance. Dirty and scratchy.' Slowly, one shallow breath at a time, her lungs relaxed, returned to doing their job properly. There *was* little resemblance to smoke in that whirl. She'd made an idiot of herself. 'Thanks for rectifying my mistake,' she whispered.

'Any time.' Sam stepped back, his hands dropping to his hips in his apparent favourite stance, taking that strength and safety with him, leaving her swaying until she found her balance, but like he was ready to catch her if necessary. That she could cope with; the intensity he was watching her with she could not.

Madison slowly looked around, taking time to get her body back under control. She was a soldier, and a doctor. No one need know she lost her cool at the sight of smoke. Or the smell of it. Or the roar of flames. Except Sam had already witnessed her near breakdown. She could only hope he wasn't going to be like a dog with a bone until he found out what that had been about.

She risked a glance at him, and gasped at the worry filling his steady summer-sky eyes.

'Are you all right?' he demanded.

'Yes.' The thudding in her chest had spread to take up residence in her skull—beat, beat, beat. She needed to get indoors, away from dust clouds—and compelling eyes that had already seen too much. 'I've never seen dust like that, and naturally…' Would he fall for this? 'Naturally I thought there was a fire. I won't make that mistake again.'

'You'd better not. It would be a hindrance on patrol. You could endanger others.' His worry didn't diminish, suggesting he was concerned she wouldn't be competent enough to do her job as a soldier.

'I think you'll find I know what I'm doing.' But reality was sinking in fast. This was nothing like practising back home, however seriously the officers had taken every manoeuvre in which they partook. If she did freak out at the sight of smoke again she might not get away with it. But as long as the camp commander didn't see fit to lock her up in a padded cell she'd be all right.

'You'd better.' His worry might be abating but he was still studying her with the intensity of a microbiologist looking down a microscope.

Which rattled her nearly as much as the dust had. Her vulnerability was rearing up again, pushing out from the corner she worked hard at keeping it tucked into. Sam—or anyone on base—must not find her lacking. Neither could he learn how insecure she could be.

'Are you sure you're okay?' he asked in a less autocratic tone.

'How long have you served on the Peninsula?' Suddenly her time here stretched before her, filled with uncertainties. Would she be strong enough to lead troops outside the camp? There'd be no respect from them if she turned into a blithering idiot because of dust. Or smoke.

'Twelve months, give or take a day.'

She'd do less. Thank goodness for something. 'Have you enjoyed your tour here?' Anything to avoid the chasm she was looking into right now.

His nod was sharp. 'This has been one of the better ones.'

'So there've been others.' Others that hadn't

been as comfortable, the edgy tone of his voice suggested.

'Yes.'

'Guess I've a lot to learn.'

'Definitely, but we all have to deal with things we're not at ease with when we first arrive. You'll be fine.' The grin was back, a little forced, but she'd accept it as it made her relax a teeny bit more. For now the danger of falling into that compelling look was far less risky than exposing the vulnerability that haunted her. This was Sam Lowe, a man she could relate to because they came from the same city, had been to the same school, and right now someone familiar was like balm on feverish skin.

*Bet he's a fantastic doctor. And a good soldier.* He'd always done well at everything he did. Yes, she remembered that much about him. The pounding behind her eyes intensified. There was too much to deal with right now. 'I need to settle into my room.' She *needed* to look forward and not back, something she couldn't manage while in Sam's presence.

'I'll see you later in the medical centre.'

She nodded. 'I'll be there as soon as possible.' And get started on her new job, even if she only got to meet her colleagues and learn the layout of the unit.

Sam turned away, spun back as though trying to catch her out. The intensity in his gaze had not backed off. Whatever he was looking for, she doubted he found it because finally he shrugged, said almost kindly, 'Welcome to the Peninsula, Maddy.' This time he strode away without a backward glance.

He remembered her friends called her Maddy? Or was it a natural abbreviation of Madison? That was more likely. He wouldn't remember much about her. Why should he? They hadn't mixed in the same crowd or been in the same classes. But… A sigh escaped her lips. The way her name sounded in his gravelly voice was something to hold onto. It warmed her when she was already hot, flattened the goose bumps that dust had raised, gave her hope. Hope for what? No idea, but it was so rare she'd hold onto it anyway.

The pack still weighed her down, pulling so

her spine curved backwards, but it was the head stuff that kept her rooted to the spot. That and the man whose long legs were eating up the parade ground as he put distance between them. She felt as though she had too many balls in the air and wasn't about to catch any of them.

Trudging towards her barracks, she tried to drag up memories of Sam. He'd been head boy in their last year, captain of his sports teams, a natural leader if the devotion from others wasn't a figment of her imagination. Officer material for sure. Which said he'd want to be in charge here in the medical unit. Probably was anyway, given he'd been here for a year.

Too much to think about right now. Exhaustion gnawed at her. Her body ached and her head was full of wool. The heat pelted her from every direction. She was in way over her depth and had no idea how to get out. But she would find a way: after a shower and a full night's sleep in a bed, and after time to reflect on how she could move forward without blotting her copybook.

Now, there was a first.

Could be quite exciting really.

# CHAPTER TWO

'MADISON HUNTER SURE grew up beautiful,' Sam muttered. But, then, she'd had a good start, had always been cute and pretty, and had kept the guys on the lookout for her around the school grounds.

Slamming the outside door behind him, he cut off the heat—and the sight of Captain Hunter. He recalled the pert nose, the sweet mouth, and the thick, dark blonde hair that had swished back and forth across her back whenever she'd worn it free of the ties that the school had insisted on most of the time. That mouth wasn't so sweet any more; tightened quickly as a lightning flash at times. But not in a sulky, spoilt manner. More as if something had hurt her in the past and she was desperate to hold herself together. There'd been a load of fear in her eyes, her face, her stance. What had that been about? Something horrendous that had changed her for ever? That'd be an explanation he could understand all too well. As for the short bob—who'd known how curly her hair was? Must've been the weight of it all that had kept it nearly straight back then.

'What had I been thinking when I rushed out to welcome her on base?' Had he wanted a taste of home? From someone who knew next to nothing about him? They were virtually strangers, had barely acknowledged each other eighteen years ago, mainly because they'd had nothing in common. These days his cocky confidence had been replaced with caution and a blinding awareness of how life could implode in an instant. Drawing everyone close to him no longer happened. Instead, he used the guilt he carried to keep everyone distant. How could he be happy when other people weren't able to be because of him?

Drawn to the window like a lad to the candy shop, he stared out at Madison dragging herself towards the officers' quarters. Tall, slim and, from the muscles tightening under his palms when he'd caught her, very fit. Enough to make a man put his heart on the line. If he had a heart. Which meant she was safe from him. He'd put that particular organ in lockdown two years ago to protect anyone from being hurt by him.

But he couldn't deny the blood in his veins. It was heating him, hardening him, reminding him how long it had been since he'd been with a woman. Too long. An oath ripped out of his mouth as the truth slam-dunked him. Unbelievable. He wanted Madison. Minutes after saying hello to someone he barely knew and he was reacting with none of the usual hesitations that instantly sprang up to protect him, and her. Unbelievable.

He was going to have to pull tight on those bands around the pit that held all his emotions. In a very short time Madison was proving to be a challenge to everything he held close and accepted as his way of life now. He'd have to dig deep to keep her off limits. But he'd had plenty of practice over the last two years, so what was one week of hardship? An impossibility? No. Definitely doable.

The window was warm against his forehead as

he tracked Maddy's slow movements. Exhaustion folded her in on herself as she hauled one shapely leg after the other. He should've taken her pack and dumped it in the barracks regardless of the fact she'd been in a hurry to get away from him. How hard would it have been to do something kind instead of walking away to save his own sanity? There was no answer. Only minutes in her company and she'd begun scrambling his brain like the eggs he'd had for breakfast.

'What's the great attraction out there?' Jock called across the room.

'Nothing,' he muttered.

'So you're going to stand there all day gaping at *nothing*?' Jock was supposedly going through patient records, removing the ones of those staff heading back to New Zealand next week.

Grabbing the interruption with both hands, he turned around. 'What's up? That stack of files doesn't appear any lower than it did an hour ago.'

Jock had probably been texting his family and pals at home. Now that they both only had a few days remaining it was getting harder to focus entirely on this tour of duty. Home was beckoning.

For him that meant another army base, another round of training as well as working in a local hospital surgical unit until the next posting. More time to contemplate the empty years ahead.

'I hear the new medic's arrived. Guess we'll meet her shortly.'

'She's unpacking.' *You're going to fall under her spell in a snap.* She was everything a red-blooded male could ask for.

'You've met her?'

'Long time back.' Yikes. He hadn't mentioned recognising her name in the email from head-quarters. Now Jock would go for his throat. Sam tried to deflect him. 'Just passed her on the field, said hello.' Had seen her become as still as a rock, colourless as marble, staring at something he'd been unable to figure out as though it was going to attack her. He'd caught her before she'd face planted. What had that been about? Smoke, she'd said. Dust, he'd told her. The fear that had blitzed him from the shadows lurking in her eyes had dampened her spark into a dark brown bog filled with hidden torments. Genuine, don't-hurt-me fear. He hated that. There'd been signs that spoke of pain and anguish, signs she'd desperately tried to hide. And failed.

*What happened to you, Madison?*

No, he didn't want to know. Knowing would lead to wanting to learn even more and before he knew it he'd be getting close to her. He'd seen that fearful look before—in William's eyes as he'd lain dying. Sam's head tipped back as pain stabbed him. William. His best friend. They'd clicked the moment they'd met on the first day of training at Papakura Military Camp. The friend who'd never returned home after following him to Afghanistan.

'Sam,' Jock called, loud enough to break into his maudlin thoughts. 'You got the hots for this woman? Or is there some juicy history?' Jock's expression was full of expectation.

*Go away, man.* But that wasn't going to happen any time soon, so Sam went for the obvious. 'I guess Madison will come visiting when she's ready,' he told the man who'd refused to back off from becoming a friend, no matter how often he'd been pushed aside.

Jock's head tipped sideways. 'Something you're not telling me?'

The guy was too shrewd for his own good. 'Can't think of anything.'

He got laughed at for his efforts. 'You've fallen for her.'

'In thirty seconds? Give me a break.' He shuddered at the thought. And that wasn't because Madison was a horror.

'I've heard that's all it takes.'

'Shouldn't you be sorting those files?'

Wrong thing to say.

'So I'm right.'

He had to shut Jock up fast. 'You couldn't be further from the mark. I cannot, will not, fall for a woman, no matter how much she interests me.'

'You ever think it time to let that go, mate?' One of Jock's eyebrows lifted nonchalantly, as if he didn't know the boundaries he was stepping over. But he did, and wasn't afraid to show it.

Heat hit Sam's cheeks as he snapped, 'Knock it off, Jock. You know the story. Nothing's changed.' Anger tightened his gut. He would never let it go. He didn't deserve happiness when William had died because of him.

Jock started to say something and Sam was instantly defensive, cutting him off. 'Don't go there,' he repeated, the warning loud and harsh in his voice. Back in New Zealand there was a woman hurting because of her fiancé's death, a lovely woman who'd never have William's children or share her life with the man she loved.

But across the room his pal merely shrugged as if this wasn't important. 'No problem. So where did you know Captain Hunter?'

'Madison. We weren't friends, just attended the same school. But there was no not knowing who she was.' Sam dragged his hand over his face. Maddy's career moves had been unbelievably similar to his. 'And don't even say we should play catch up on people we might both have known at school. I'm not interested so I'm staying out of her way as much as possible for the time I've got left here.' As the words were spilling regret flicked through his jaded psyche. He wanted to spend time with her despite the restrictions he'd imposed upon himself. But he'd stay away. One week wasn't too long to hold out on this strange need to touch base with her sneaking through him. One week.

'You seen the roster for tomorrow's patrol?' There was a mischievous sparkle in Jock's eyes that didn't bode well for his vow to stay clear of trouble.

Dread he didn't understand floored him. One look at the notice board partially explained. 'Swap with me.' Maddy had problems. He'd seen them in her eyes, in that fear, and for him to get involved, maybe help her, would endanger both of them. Ultimately he'd let her down, one way or another. He did that to people who mattered to him. Never again. 'Please,' he grunted. Not quite begging, but damned close.

'No can do. I'm rostered to take my crew into town and check out the hot spots there.'

'So swap.'

'Nope.' Jock shook his craggy head. 'Captain Hunter's all yours.'

Sam's crew would be patrolling beyond the town's perimeters. 'That sucks. She'd better be up to scratch,' was all he could come up with, though he didn't understand his concerns. Neither did he understand why his fingertips tingled and his groin ached just thinking about her.

Like he was eighteen all over again, working hard to be Mr Popularity at school, to show it didn't matter he was being raised by a family that was unrelated to him because his own had left him. A wonderful, kind and caring family, but not his.

Jock clapped a hand on his shoulder. 'These next few days could prove interesting. Time I witnessed you being brought to your knees over a woman.'

'You going to let up on this any time soon?' The guy knew what had gone down in Sam's past so why all this bull dust?

A low cry came from the treatment room, cutting through his gloom. He raised an eyebrow at Jock. 'One of ours?'

Jock shook his head. 'That's the mother of a three-year-old boy with five rotten teeth and inflamed gums. They were brought in while you were out filling the gas tanks.'

So he hadn't been texting. 'You never mentioned them when I came back.' Or when he'd started out to welcome Madison.

Jock shrugged. 'You want to swap anything, you can take this one for me.'

'Where are you up to with the boy?' Sam held out a hand for the notes being extended in his direction.

'Waiting on bloods before putting him out so as we can extract what's left of his teeth.' Jock fidgeted with other files on his table. Everyone knew he hated working with children, found it too stressful since losing a child in an emergency operation under extreme conditions in Afghanistan two years ago. He'd been on a hiding to nothing before he'd even picked up the scalpel but no one had been able to make him see that then or afterwards.

Sam could've asked to change places on patrol in return for taking over the boy's case and Jock probably would've obliged but, damn it, he wouldn't do that to his pal. All right, Jock was a pal, was getting closer all the time, but not so close Sam would hurt him. Good to have him at his back, though.

'Would you look at that?' Jock's eyes were so wide he appeared blinded by bright lights.

Sam didn't have to turn in the direction his mate was staring to know Maddy had entered the room, way earlier than he'd expected. 'She's quite something, isn't she?'

'Can see why you were mooning at the window.'

'I wasn't mooning.'

Jock's head bobbed like a balloon on the water. 'You sure you don't want to stay on for the next six months?' he cracked.

Sam laughed, if that's what the strangled sound that burst from his mouth was. Bitter, dry and full of despair. 'I'm no good for her.' But he had to face up to her—now and again and again over the coming days—without becoming mesmerised by her. He turned to nod abruptly at Madison. 'That was quick.' Some colour had returned to her cheeks, but the exhaustion remained.

'The shower was cold.' Her shrug was defensive.

'That happens around here.' Relief softened

him. Her fear had backed off. He doubted it was gone, but right now she wasn't being crippled by it. Wariness now met his gaze. Was she worried he'd told everyone she'd freaked out over a dust cloud? Not a chance. 'Cold water's just another thing to get used to. Come and meet the crew. Jock, Madison Hunter.'

Jock was on his feet in an instant, his hand extended in greeting. 'Hey, great to have you on board. Sam says you two know each other from school.'

Her mouth twisted into something resembling a smile. Not her old full-on, love-me-or-get-out-of-my-space smile, but something softer and more cautious that inexplicably settled over Sam's heart, loosened some of the tension he wore twenty-four seven. She said, 'That's an exaggeration.' She might've been talking to Jock but those weary eyes were on him. 'I didn't play rugby and Sam wasn't into debating.'

'You still do that? Belong to a debating team, I mean.' Damned if he could turn away. It felt as though he was falling into a pit, a deep one filled with the scent of home, the warmth of people he'd grown up with, the lure of a future he'd denied himself too long. And would continue to deny himself. But he would not hide from Madison for the next week. Decision made, he closed the gap between them. 'You used to be very good.'

'At arguing a point?' Her mouth softened. 'I still argue about most things, but no longer under the guise of representing a team.'

'You sure Sam wasn't in your team?' Jock filled the sudden silence developing between Madison and Sam and halting the prickly sensation tripping down Sam's spine. 'He's always disputing everything around here.'

'Really?' Those brown eyes widened, lightened into the colour of his favourite milk chocolate. 'So you know better than the army?' she teased.

'Don't tell the commander.' He grinned.

'As if he doesn't know,' Jock quipped, before heading towards the room where his young patient waited.

'I said I'd take that case,' Sam called after him.

He needed to get out of here anyway. 'You give Maddy the rundown on how the clinic works.'

'No, you do that.' Damn the guy but he'd shut the door on anything else Sam had to say.

'What case?' Maddy asked. 'Can I do something to help?'

'No, everything's under control. Anyway, you're not fit for duty until you've had some sleep.'

'I guess. One of the troops unwell?' She didn't let a subject drop easily.

'A child was brought in to have teeth removed.' Now she'd really crank up the questions.

'One of those waiting outside earlier? I thought you said they weren't allowed in very often.'

'There are exceptions. Especially with children.'

'I'm glad.' Her hand hovered over her stomach. 'Kids shouldn't be denied treatment because of the adult world around them.'

'Agreed.' He took a long breath, pushed aside thoughts of children and babies, especially those he'd once hoped he might have with a special woman he could give his heart to. When Maddy opened her mouth he rushed to close her down before she said something that might have him saying things he told no one. 'You like kids?'

That hand flattened hard against her belly. The fingers whitened they were so tense. 'Adore them.' Her voice quivered.

Why? What was going on? Things weren't adding up. Earlier she'd been terrified of smoke that hadn't been smoke, now there was a distinct hint of sadness in her expression. 'So do I,' Sam commented, still wondering if Madison had problems at home. There were no rings on her fingers. Her surname hadn't changed. 'You haven't married or got into a full-time relationship?' he asked, oh, so casually, so as not to wind her up.

'Divorced and single,' she muttered after a long minute contemplating the wall behind him.

He hadn't realised he'd been holding his breath until he heard those words. Would've been better if she was hooked up with someone. Then he'd be able to laugh at this annoying sense of wanting to get closer to her. He'd never step on another man's patch. What did that matter when he had no intention of having a relationship at all? 'I'm sorry to hear that. About the divorce, I mean,' he added quickly, in case she misinterpreted his comment.

'So was I. At the time.' Then she winced. No doubt thinking she'd said far too much about herself. 'Shall we go and see if we can help Jock?'

'Sure.' The boy did not need three doctors but Sam needed to get back on track with keeping away from Maddy, and she, he suspected, needed a diversion after revealing something so painful. The divorce must've been something she hadn't wanted. Had she got over it? For her sake, he hoped so. Wasting life pining for what might've been would be a shame, thought the expert at it.

# CHAPTER THREE

'NEED SOME BLOOD HERE,' Sam called from the other side of the treatment room six hours later.

At the sound of the deep voice that brought images of pebbles rolling up the beach on a wave Madison looked up to find Sam watching her. 'You want me to get it?' When she already had her hands full?

His headshake was abrupt. 'You carry on extracting that bullet.'

'I'm on to it.' Literally. The forceps she held tapped against metal deep in her patient's thigh right on cue. Maddy grimaced. Talk about being thrown in at the deep end. Removing a bullet from this man's thigh wasn't difficult, but it was different from anything she'd dealt with in emergency departments back home. Which could explain why Sam had given her this patient when they'd been called in from the barracks. Getting her up to speed ASAP. Bullets and the army went hand in hand, she just hadn't thought she'd be facing any this soon. She'd wanted something outside her comfort zone, and now it looked like she'd got it.

He seemed to have to pull his gaze away from her to call out, 'Cassy, a bag of O neg wouldn't go amiss here.'

'Coming right up,' replied the nurse she'd met half an hour ago when she'd raced in dressed in a hurriedly pulled on long T and shorts.

One wide-eyed stare from Sam and she'd also hauled on scrubs quick smart. He had no idea of the hideous sight her garments covered, and the scrubs would make doubly sure neither he nor anyone else did find out. 'What's up?' she'd asked at the time to nudge his attention away from her. Just in case Sam had X-ray vision and could see through her clothes.

He'd brought her up to speed fast. 'Three locals were brought to the main entrance with injuries sustained when a man in the market went berserk with a gun. You've got the thigh wound.'

'Not a problem,' she'd replied, and had ignored

his muttered comment that had gone something like 'nor should it be'.

'We have stocks of blood on hand?' Maddy asked now. 'Seriously?' This wasn't a fully equipped hospital with all the bells and whistles. Neither was there a blood bank to draw from.

'We keep a small supply on hand. The troops donate as it's required.'

'I guess we're lucky the gunman wasn't a very good shot or there'd have been more casualties,' she said, dropping the bullet into a stainless steel dish with a clang.

'The hospital in town will be busy with other victims,' Sam explained. 'We get those who're prepared to make the uncomfortable trip out here.' He paused cleansing the gaping wound on his patient's head and watched as she sutured her patient's laceration. 'Very tidy.'

Her hackles rose. Did he think she wouldn't do a good job? Of course he wouldn't know she was a perfectionist. Lifting her eyes, she drew a quick breath. The face looking at her was devoid of rancour, filled only with admiration. 'Thank you,' she muttered, bewildered, and waited for the axe to fall.

'So sewing's one of your talents.' His smile was soft, not egotistic or antagonistic. Apparently genuine. Even friendly.

Which worried her more than an abrasive style would've. 'It wasn't until I went to med school.'

'You wouldn't have had to make your own clothes when you were growing up.' Now he grinned in what was becoming a familiar way.

'Nope. Does anyone these days?' she asked. She was softening more and more towards him, and she hadn't been here twenty-four hours yet. Hard not to when he was playing nice, when her arms still had memories of those strong hands keeping her from dropping to the ground earlier. So much for remaining aloof to safeguard herself from rejection. The first rejection had decimated her. She'd never get up from a second blow. Come on, Sam was only being friendly, nothing else.

'Not me, for one. I let the army choose my clothes.'

She aimed for light. 'Not Paris fashion, are they?'

'Now, that's something I know nothing about,' he drawled.

'Me either.' But her mother dressed superbly from high end shops. Madison came from money and that had caused grief at school from some of the small-minded sorts. Shame none of those imbeciles had bothered to learn how hard she'd worked during out-of-school hours before mouthing off about her family. 'But I admit to having an interesting wardrobe back home.' A fantastic collection of outfits her mother had bought her and which were totally impractical in her day-to-day life. Something to do with getting back out amongst the city folk and finding a new man apparently.

Maddy shuddered. Not happening. This time because she'd learned how fickle love truly was. One glimpse of her scars and Jason had come up with every excuse in the book to bail on their marriage. Sure, he'd taken a few months—long, dark, lonely months—but in the end he'd gone. And he'd supposedly loved her. What she'd never got around to telling him was that her chances of having children had been severely compromised as well. What had been the point? She hadn't wanted him staying because he'd felt sorry for her.

*Focus, Maddy. That's history.*

Continuing to suture the wound in front of her, she stifled a yawn. So much for getting some sleep before her tour got fully under way. Who was she kidding? Her head had been full of Sam Lowe, dust and smoke, Sam, burns, and more Sam. Digging for a bullet had been a welcome reprieve.

Sam was staring at her, lifting goose bumps on her skin and unexpected, unneeded hope in her belly. 'You okay?' he asked.

'Yes.' She stared right back, her breath hitched somewhere between her lungs and her nostrils. The deeper she looked into that well the harder it was to find the strength to ignore him. The same concern she'd seen in the midst of her meltdown over the smoke blinked at her. Which was plain scary. Could she manage to work alongside him without falling into the trap of wanting him? *You don't already?* That's why she had to keep him at arm's length. This yearning for Sam was growing, not in great dollops but it was there, moving in under her skin, raising her temperature degree by agonising degree, shaking her need to remain immune to men until cracks were beginning to appear.

Cassy nudged Sam. 'One bag of cells for your man.'

His gaze appeared to drag across Maddy's face, a soft caress, as though loth to leave, then he flicked his head sideways to eyeball the nurse. The syringe in his left hand was in danger of snapping as he stepped back from the bed. 'Get a line in, will you?'

'No problem.'

Maddy dropped her eyes to her patient, focusing on his wound but unable to push Sam out of her mind. That need he'd brought to her expanded around her determination to ignore it, swamped all ideas of staying immune to him in particular, frightening *and* exciting her. Forget the excitement. How? Remember the horror in Jason's eyes the first time he'd seen her burned abdomen. That particular image could always toughen her resolve like nothing else could.

'How's the third victim doing?' she heard Sam ask through the mess in her head.

Cassy answered, 'Went into cardiac arrest but Jock got him back. You think your man needed blood. Not even close.'

'We need a volunteer to give a pint?'

Maddy looked up at Sam's question. 'I'm O neg, if you need it.'

'We're good to go at the moment.' The nurse slid a needle into Sam's patient's arm. 'Righto, my man, let's get you hooked up and these little red cells doing their job.'

Madison let the words wash over her. Operating rooms were the same wherever she went, and as close to home as she knew these days. Listening to the banter, suturing a shredded muscle was soothing in an odd kind of way.

Sam had gone quiet. A flick of her eyes showed him working on his patient's scalp where the man had taken a pounding from an unknown object. His attention was so focused on the job that he had to be trying very hard to ignore something.

It wouldn't be her, surely? Hopefully not. Yet a shaft of disappointment jabbed. Disappointment she refused to delve into. Instead, she hunted for a bland question and came up with, 'Where are you headed next week, Sam?'

'Burwood.'

The military base near Christchurch. 'Really going home, then, huh?'

'Until the brass find some other place to send me.'

'When was the last time you spent any time there?'

At first she didn't think he was going to answer but finally he managed, 'Ages ago. I haven't seen Ma and Pa Creighton for far too long.' Guilt lined his words and filled his eyes.

'Who are they?'

'They took me in to live with them when I was fourteen. The kindest folk you'd ever want to know.'

And he hadn't been to see them for a while. She knew not to ask about that, and for once managed to keep quiet. Not that she stopped wondering what had happened that he'd needed a home back then. Where had his parents been? Had he been a welfare kid? She knew about them as when she'd been young her parents had fostered two boys slightly older than her whom she'd adored and had been devastated when they'd left to return to their families.

Then Sam interrupted her fruitless machinations. 'Why did you join up?'

'I was looking for something different to the usual track of building a big, fancy career in a private practice.' She'd wanted out of her life as it had become. At least until she could face a future without the husband and children she'd always dreamed of.

'That had been your initial goal?'

'Yes. Then I had a change of mind.' A near death experience could do that.

'Going to tell me why?'

'No.' Then she added, before she could overthink it, 'Not now.' Explaining about the fire and the ensuing disaster would be hard. But hard didn't begin to explain the consequences that had followed that terrifying night. 'I guess eventually I'll go back to that idea but not yet.' But would she?

The army had taken her away from home and the hideous memories, from her concerned family with their endless suggestions of how to get back on track. There were awful memories ground so deep she'd never expunge them, but they were slightly easier to ignore when she wasn't living and working in her home town. Something she owed her sister for. She wouldn't have chosen the army as a cure if not for Maggie's suggestion—nagging, more like—that it could be a way to reinvent herself. She'd grabbed that thought and signed up without thinking too hard about what she was letting herself in for. Desperation made people do strange things.

On the plus side, her body was fitter, more muscular and in the best shape it had ever been. Her smart mind was faster, sharper, and yet only now was it dawning on her what she had landed herself in.

*So much for being intelligent. Hope I haven't messed up big time.*

Too bad if she had. The only way out of here

was by court-martial or in a wooden box. Not options worthy of consideration. Yet she was supposed to be getting over horrors, not facing new ones. By the end of her tour, far from the comfort of home and her well-meaning but over-protective family, she fully intended knowing what she wanted to do with the rest of her life, and the past would be exactly that. The past. That was the plan anyway. Except plans had a way of going off track.

'I hear uncertainty in that answer.' No challenge sparked in the eyes now locked on her. Instead curiosity ruled.

Her natural instinct was to pull down the shutters. Habit was a strong taskmaster. Since the fire, she was done with showing anything but the truth, even a watered-down version, so she usually kept quiet. But now she was starting over? Straightening her already straight spine, she said, 'I haven't got any long-term plans at the moment. I'm taking everything one day at a time. Or one tour anyway.' Now she'd said too much.

He nodded, said quietly, 'You and I have something in common.'

Hideous memories? Pain? Fear? She hoped not. She didn't wish bad things on him. 'You aren't going to be a soldier for ever?'

'No idea. I had planned on it, but now who knows?'

That sounded lame, but before she could ask Sam to expand on what he'd said Jock appeared in their cramped area.

Sam looked down at his patient. 'Think we're about done. You?'

'The guy didn't make it.'

Madison's head flicked back and forth between the two men, then she locked on Sam. 'This isn't uncommon, is it?'

'Losing a patient? No.' That get-me-anything smile was back in place, but his serious voice didn't match it. Could be Sam was hiding his own despair at what they dealt with.

Hairs lifted on her neck. 'Sam?' His name fell out of her mouth.

'You're in a brutal environment now, Madison.'

Phew. He thought she was thinking about the medical work. Better than him knowing the truth. 'I get that,' she replied.

He went on. 'It takes time to get used to the injuries we see here, especially what causes them, but if you don't you'll sink.'

'I'm hardly likely to do that.' She could feel her muscles tightening. Stop it. New approach, remember? No more getting uptight over everything. Forcing the tension aside, she tried for normal. 'But thanks for the warning. I'll be on guard.'

'You'd better be. For all our sakes.' His words were sharp, but the smile that accompanied them lessened any suspected blow. It was genuine, not full of I'm-so-cool attitude.

'You'll have to trust me on this, Sam.' Huh? That was a big ask. There wasn't room for trust in manoeuvres with an unproven soldier. That's how people died, or so the training officers back home had hammered home.

Sam's smile faltered, slid away. 'I will.' Forceps clanged against the steel of a kidney dish, loud in the sudden silence. 'But if you find you're struggling I'm not bad at listening.'

Now, there was an offer she'd have to decline. Talking one on one with Sam with no one else around about personal concerns would be taking things way too far. Shame. It could be good to sit over a coffee and chat about life in general, learn a few snippets about what made him tick. There was a depth to him that drew her in, intrigued her. 'Strange how real life is way different from those lofty ideas I had at school. Nothing turns out as sweet and easy as it looked then.'

Grief shot through his eyes, darkening them to a dull, wintry day. There was a storm in there, swirling emotions moving too fast to catch. 'Time we talked about something else, Madison.' There was no force behind his words, just a low, please-stop-this tone.

'Fair enough,' she answered equally quietly, more than happy to oblige. But what sore had she scratched?

'You caved too easily.' He stepped away from the bed, rolling his shoulders, pulling up a grin that didn't fit quite right.

Aha. He definitely hid behind that mouth, those grins. 'Lack of sleep catching up.'

'That explains why you've also gone quiet,'

Sam gulped around another grin. 'You sure you're who I think you are?'

'Probably not.' She wasn't recognising herself at the moment.

He came around the bed to stand directly in front of her. His finger tilted her chin so she had to meet his gaze. The intimacy of the gesture shocked her, but she didn't want to pull away. Waiting for him to say whatever was on his mind made her nervous. Her jaws locked, while her brain spilled words she struggled not to utter.

His finger slid over her jaw before he removed his hand and stepped back. 'I like having someone from my time at Christchurch High School turn up here. That was a good place in my life and you've brought back memories even if you weren't involved.'

Her head spun. 'You haven't kept in touch with guys from school?'

'Not really. I couldn't wait to get out of town at the time, not realising how lucky I was to live there.'

'So visiting Christchurch doesn't happen often?'

Sam shook his head at her. 'Unfortunately not. Life has a tendency to throw curve balls just when I think I'm ready to go back there and maybe look into setting up a practice.' Those summer-blue eyes quickly darkened back to winter.

'Well, well. I sure hit the nail on the head earlier.' Jock stood beside them, looking from her to Sam and back.

'Can it,' Sam snapped. His shoulders were back to tight, and straighter than a ruler. His jaw pushed forward, and the winter in his gaze kicked up an ice storm.

'If you're done, let's grab a coffee,' Jock said as though nothing out of the ordinary had gone down.

The glove Sam was removing tore as he tugged it. 'Nah. You entertain our new medic. I've got things to do.'

Contrition caught Madison. She didn't know if she'd contributed to upsetting him, but she regretted it if she had. 'Sam, I don't understand what's going on but, whatever it is, I am sorry.'

'You haven't put a foot wrong.' He stared at her,

a war going on in his face. 'The thing is, Madison, I'm at the end of my tour of duty, you're at the beginning.' He swallowed hard. 'So good luck. You're going to need it.' He turned and stormed out of the room.

Madison stared after him, regret at his abrupt departure swamping her. 'What just happened?'

Jock shrugged. 'Welcome to the Peninsula. It does strange things to the sanest of us at times. Sam will be his usual self by sun-up.' But his gaze was worried as he stared after his friend.

Sam did three laps of the perimeter, walking hard and fast. His breathing was rapid, while his body dripped with sweat despite the cooler night air.

'Damn it, Madison, get out of my head.' He didn't want her lurking in there, reminding him of the future he'd once longed for. The future that had held a wife and family, people to shower with love, to protect and give himself to. The future that was no longer his to have.

He looked around, hoped no one had heard his outburst. Only went to show what a state

Maddy's arrival had got him into if he was talking to himself out loud. Might get locked up if the wrong person overheard him. A week in the cells would keep him clear of Madison. Now, that could be a plus.

Why had the arrival of Maddy, someone he'd barely known so long ago, flipped up all the pain and anguish he kept hidden deep within himself?

Stopping his mad charge, he leaned a shoulder against the fence, drawing in deep gulps of sticky air. None of this ranting was helping. This was when he missed his pal the most, missed venting about things that stirred him up.

William had filled a gap in his life in a similar way to how Ma and Pa Creighton had filled in for his mother when she'd died. Sam's skin tightened. The guilt he'd carried over his friend's death stymied everything he thought he might do next with his life. Having fun when his friend was beyond it was not possible. Finding happiness with a woman was undeserved and to be avoided at all costs in case he ruined it for her.

Sam shoved away from the fence, began jogging, his shoes slapping the hard soil and raising dust.

Voices and laughter beckoned as he passed the open door of the officers' canteen where the rest of the crew, including Madison, would be drinking tea and eating cookies to replace the nervous energy they'd expended in Theatre. Operating on victims of gunfire or a bombing made everyone uneasy, reminding them why the army was there. Reminding them all that any one of them could be the next on the operating table. He should be in there, relaxing, cracking jokes, putting the day to bed, not out here, winding himself into a knot of apprehension.

He continued jogging.

Until his heart lurched, forcing his legs to slow then stop. A harsh laugh escaped him. He'd been so busy thinking about Madison he hadn't seen her in the shadows laid across the ground from the mess building. She shuffled across the parade ground, her arms hanging at her sides, her chin resting on her sternum. Close to lifeless.

'Hey,' he whispered softly, almost afraid she'd hear and straighten up, put strength back in her muscles and pretend she was fine. The picture before him was honest, and punched him in the gut. This was a new picture. One thing he did remember was that Maddy had always been energy personified. Not right at this moment, though. Neither had she been earlier when she'd come off that plane.

*Oh, Maddy, what has happened to you?*

A shaft of pain sliced into him. For her. He didn't want her suffering, hurting, crying on the inside.

Madison paused her slow progress, glanced around. Had she heard his footfalls on the dirt? Was she aware of him? She took a couple of steps. Guess not. Then she stopped again, leaned back and stared up at the sky where a myriad of stars sparkled. Her hands lifted to her hips as she gazed upwards. The outline of her breasts aiming skyward forced the air out of his lungs.

Beautiful. Even in her overtired state she was the most alluring woman he'd come across, from that attractive short hair right down to the tips of her boots.

Sam spun away, trying to fling the ache she'd

created from his body. Another circuit of the camp might fix what ailed him, though running in his current state would be a novelty. He turned back to look at Maddy again. *Call her Madison. Maddy's too intimate, too friendly.* Yet it was all he wanted to call her.

'You done beating yourself up?' Jock strolled into his line of vision, hands shoved into his pockets and a sympathetic smile on his face. 'Feel like a beer?'

'Thought you'd never ask.' Two in the morning and they were talking about having a beer. How messed up were they? 'We've got patrol at zero eight hundred hours.'

'Then we'd better get on with it.'

The beer wasn't going to happen. They'd settle for a mug of tea followed by a few hours' kip, and he'd wake to a new day that didn't include X-rated pictures of Madison Hunter. Wouldn't he?

A shiver rattled Sam as she continued strolling away towards the barracks. His body was giving him messages he had to knock down. He was not getting close to her. Not now. Not ever. So he'd treat her as he did everyone else around here, as a fellow soldier and doctor, and see where that led. Hopefully out of the she's-so-sexy-I-could-cry slot and into the just-another-medic category.

Slam. There it was—a mental picture of Madison standing in the middle of the medical unit, looking good enough to eat.

And he was hungry. Starved, in fact.

But the past went wherever he went, haunting in its persistence, preventing him moving on and grabbing life's chances. Painful when he thought about all he could've had, and would never obtain. He was not entitled to love and happiness ever after. He'd thrown that away with William's life.

Why the surprise? It wasn't as though he didn't know better. His mother had told him never to trust anyone with his heart after his dad had ditched them in an old shack by the river in one of Christchurch's less than savoury districts.

Sam knew how these things worked, had always known, yet he'd still carried a thread of hope in his heart. Ma and Pa Creighton had shown love and happiness were possible when they'd taken him, a sulky kid with no credentials except how to shoplift with impunity, into their home and family and given him a chance. He'd believed them, in them.

Until his friend had died. That had been reality kicking him in the gut, reminding him he'd been wrong to think he could have it all.

# CHAPTER FOUR

'IF THAT FLY doesn't go away quick smart I'm going to smash it with the back of my hand,' Madison muttered under her breath. But she didn't move, not a hair. The blasted fly kept crawling across her face.

She scoped the landscape for anomalies, her back to the dilapidated concrete block building her patrol was inspecting from a hundred metres. Her hands gripped the weapon she held hard against her body. The silence was excruciating. The lack of movement was scary, and a warning in itself. The air hummed with tension as soldiers waited, watching and analysing everything around them. They'd just received info of insurgents hiding out in what used to be a police station and was now a ruin after being bombed last year.

'Cop, Porky, move in.' Sam spoke in a low

voice that didn't carry beyond the troops. 'You three...' he pointed to the soldiers beside Madison '...take the left. Captain Hunter, you're with me and Jerry on the right.'

Sam was checking her out, otherwise it would've made more sense for her to go left with the others. He'd been observing her all day and it bugged her. Of course he wanted to know if she was up to speed on a mission, but did he have to be so obvious? She wouldn't have been sent here if she couldn't do her job.

Madison scanned the landscape once more before following Sam and Jerry. Movement caught her attention. 'Wait,' she called softly. 'Five o'clock, inbound, one person, on his belly.'

Every soldier paused. Sam was instantly beside her, moving fast without appearing to. He followed the direction of her gaze and nodded once, abruptly. 'Well spotted, Captain.'

She ignored the glow of satisfaction warming her. She was only doing her job, and proving she was capable of it, but there'd been a hint of respect in Sam's voice that she couldn't ignore. It touched her when she didn't want to be touched by him. If words could do that, what damage would physical connection do to her stability?

'Ah!' She stifled a cry. No one put a hand on her these days without having it swiped away. Imagine Sam spreading his hand, palm down, on her stomach, on the warped skin. Nausea swarmed up her throat.

'Captain?' Sam growled softly.

Gulp. 'We still going inside?' she asked.

'After we've checked out that crawling body, established whether they're friend or foe, we'll reconnoitre.' He nodded at the two men beside him, pointed where he wanted them to go. 'Cop, Porky, hold your positions and keep watch over the police block.'

What was it with all these nicknames? Porky was thinner than a broom handle. Madison scanned the ground all the way up to that small person they were targeting. Nothing else stood out. She checked to the left, the right. 'All clear.'

'We'll run opposite Porky and Cop,' Sam told her, and immediately was on his feet, running in a crouch, his weapon ready.

Madison followed, matching him step for step,

her eyes constantly scanning for anything out of the ordinary. Nothing was remarkable, and yet nothing was normal when compared to what she knew back home. 'I think it's a child.'

Sam stopped, took in what she'd observed through binoculars. 'A lad. Don't be fooled. He could be as dangerous as any adult you'll come across.' He flicked his hand at his side to get the attention of the soldiers on their left flank, pointed to the boy.

Cop raised a thumb, and they all moved forward slowly, expectantly, until Sam and Madison reached the boy, who immediately spread his arms and legs starfish style in the dirt.

Madison dropped to her knees, reached out a hand.

'Don't touch him,' Sam growled. 'He could be carrying.'

The boy cried out a torrent of words that Madison couldn't comprehend. A glance at Sam told her he was none the wiser.

'Now what?'

Sam didn't get a chance to reply. The boy flipped his clothes up to expose bare skin underneath. He wasn't carrying. Could be he was just a normal kid doing what kids everywhere did, playing in the dirt. A very dangerous place for games, if the warnings she'd heard were true. And why wouldn't they be? The soldiers who'd been stationed on base for the previous year knew first-hand what went on out here.

The air whistled across Madison's lips. 'Thank goodness.'

'Stay with him, soldier. Be alert,' Sam commanded Jerry before moving away.

*Thump.* A low explosive sound broke through the silence from behind the building, followed by a gut-twisting cry.

After checking they were safe, Sam raced around the corner, Madison on his heels.

'Man down.' She stated the obvious the moment she saw past Sam.

'Cover us,' Sam ordered, and fell to his knees. 'Porky, you okay?'

'It's his foot. Something exploded under him,' Cop told them.

'Take Captain Hunter's place. Don't forget

there could be more out there,' Sam ordered. 'Madison, give me a hand here.'

Instantly she knelt on the opposite side of Porky, glancing around before focusing on their patient. His left boot was shredded, as was his foot from what she could see. Tugging off her pack, she pulled out the emergency first aid kit, tugged on gloves and found thick gauze pads to help staunch the bleeding.

Sam helped himself to more gloves then began assessing Porky's injury. 'Hang in there, Sergeant. I'm going to have a look at the damage. Okay?'

'Figured as much.' The soldier bit down hard as Sam began probing his wound.

'We need the helicopter,' Madison said. 'I'll call it in.'

'Do that.' Sam leaned closer to her, said quietly, 'I suspect he's going to lose that foot unless he's very lucky.'

'His luck ran out when he got hit.' She called base and quickly explained the situation. 'They're on their way,' she told Sam and Porky.

'This damned dust doesn't help,' Sam muttered as he tried to protect the site of the wound.

'You warned me it got everywhere.' Porky needed to get to Theatre urgently, or be in sterile conditions at the very least.

Sam flicked her a warm glance. 'Yeah, and this would have to be a bad scenario.' He found the morphine in the kit and drew up a dose, glancing over at her before administering the drug into Porky's thigh. Then he spoilt her focus. 'You haven't been confused into thinking it's smoke today?'

'No.' She shuddered. Made to touch her belly where the scars were tingling, stopped just in time. Or had she? Sam's eyes were following her gesture. 'I only make any mistake once.' Or tried to. Making an idiot of herself on patrol was not an option. The soldiers would never trust her as their leader when Sam left. Yesterday had been a timely lesson. Dust, not smoke. She'd gone to sleep saying it. She'd come close to tripping up today when she'd seen thin lines of real smoke spiralling from dwellings, but with Sam keeping a close eye on her she'd managed not to lose her grip and to smother her unease. So far he had no cause for concern about her behaviour while on patrol that she knew of.

Porky's face turned grey. Sweat covered his pallid cheeks. Shock had set in. Madison lifted his eyelid. 'Pupils dilated.' She took his wrist in her hand, felt for a pulse. 'Weak and rapid.'

'Trying to clean this is hopeless.'

Madison swabbed at the ankle, cleaning away blood and sand, constantly aware of the broken bones, and the pain too much pressure could cause. 'We can't do a lot out here except keep him comfortable.'

'I need to bind the foot as tightly as possible,' Sam said. 'Hand me the gauze. It'll do the trick.'

She dug through the bag and came up with a large roll that would go round Porky's foot and lower leg several times. 'This'll work.'

The wonderful sound of rotors beating up the air reached them, and Madison relaxed back onto her heels. 'Thank goodness for the cavalry.'

'I second that.'

It took only moments to lift Porky onto the stretcher and into the belly of the helicopter.

'A well-oiled team,' she muttered.

Sam tossed her emergency kit in and turned to her. 'Up you get. Someone has to go with Porky and I've got a team to bring back to base after we've gone through the police block.'

'I could do that,' she retorted, then wished her words back. 'Sorry, you do know your way around far better than me.'

'Yes, Madison, I do. We also still have a boy to escort away from here.' Then his mouth tipped into a smile, a friendly one. She was getting used to those. Had started looking for them. 'Besides, you've had more than your share of drama since arriving less than twenty-four hours ago. Take the ride, and make the most of it. It doesn't happen often.'

'That's something to be grateful for.' She found herself returning his smile. 'Not needing one of our own to be cas-vaced out, I mean.'

'I knew exactly what you meant. Now go. The flight crew don't like hanging around, too dangerous. Especially when we don't know who might be loitering beyond the building.'

'Be careful.' Please. *I'd hate for something to*

*happen to you.* She leapt on board, helped by the waiting hands of the co-pilot who then pointed to the bucket seat that was hers for the few minutes it would take to reach base. Looking out the gap where a door used to be, she saw Sam, hands on hips, staring after the helicopter as it rose, flinging sand and dirt at everyone on the ground. For a brief moment his gaze locked with hers, creating chaos in her stomach and beyond. Defrosting more of the ice that had been in her belly and the back of her mind for far too long.

Then the chopper was too high to see him and she shuffled her butt back in the uncomfortable seat to watch over their patient, who'd drifted into shock-induced unconsciousness. Reaching for Porky's wrist, she again took note of his rapid pulse rate and the pallor of his skin, all the while thinking about those fierce yet kind blue eyes that showed a side of Sam she didn't want to acknowledge for fear of where they might lead her.

*I might find I like Sam Lowe too much.*

Now, there was a worry. But what harm could liking the guy do? Plenty. For starters, there were those unwanted moments when her body reacted favourably to his. Favourably? What was this? A weather report? More like hungrily. She wanted Sam. There. She'd admitted it. No going back on her thoughts. Which kind of made becoming only friends difficult, if not impossible, unless she found a way to banish the intense physical yearning that had begun unfurling yesterday. They would not be getting close in any way. She simply didn't have the courage required to expose her body.

The day she'd seen those scars disfiguring her torso for the first time had altered her for ever. The pain from the burns had had nothing on the agony that new view had created. It'd taken nearly six weeks before she could look again, a sneaky peek at the ugliness that was the new her. It had been worse that time. Her shocked memory from her first viewing of the scars had not been honest. The horror and despair had floored her that day; while her strength had deserted her over the months spent fighting one infection after another in a cloud of pain. Sometimes she'd been conscious, at others she had been blissfully unaware of anything going on around her.

If she ever considered anything so stupid as to want to strip down naked with a man, she only had to bring Jason to the front of her mind. The revulsion in his eyes when he'd inadvertently seen her burns had scarred her more than the fire had. He'd tried to hide it, deny it, but, hey, she'd seen the same look in her own face the day before so had instantly recognised it for what it was.

Nowadays there were moments when she thought if only she had the guts to move on, not care what anyone thought, she might actually find a man who loved her enough not to give a damn about a bit of damaged skin. Looking through the helicopter's opening, she scanned the sky for a miracle. Nope. Nothing.

*Thought so. You have to love yourself before you can ask anyone else to.*

She stared outside again, looking for the source of that whacky idea. Nothing. No dragons slaying beasts, no witches on broomsticks chasing away black clouds.

The helicopter nudged onto the landing pad outside the hospital unit on base, jolting Madison back to reality, refocusing her attention to shifting Porky without causing him any more distress.

'You don't take time to settle in before everything turns belly up, do you?' Jock was clambering inside the aircraft.

'I'm hoping I've seen the worst for a while,' she tossed over her shoulder as she raised Porky's eyelid. 'No one home.'

'Probably for the best until we're inside. Fill me in on the details while we shift him.'

She did, leaving nothing out. 'Sam's still patrolling that area around the old police station. He wasn't convinced the area was clear of insurgents, and there's a boy to see clear of the site.'

'I'm surprised he didn't take the flight and leave you out there.' There was an irritating smile on Jock's face. 'He's always the first to put newbies under pressure, and there's no pressure like your first patrol when something goes wrong.'

So Sam had been kind to her. Her mouth lifted into a smile.

'What?' Jock asked.

'Maybe Sam thinks I'm more use to Porky than he might be.' Huh?

Jock spluttered with laughter. 'Tell me you're joking.'

'I'm joking. Why?'

'Because Sam is a brilliant surgeon and knows it. Believe me when I say he was doing you a favour.'

'Truly?' Gobsmacked just about described her. Damn it, Sam was starting a thaw deep inside her that she didn't want to end until all the frost had gone. One day after arriving here and he was inadvertently encouraging her to look outward, not inside all the time. Which only spelt danger. She might become enthralled with him, even go so far as to fall in love with him. In a week? Why not? There were a hundred reasons. Her heart wouldn't withstand another bludgeoning. It hadn't recovered from the first one.

'Truly.' Jock laughed at her.

It wasn't hard to find a return smile for Jock. He was one of the good guys. 'Hadn't we better get cracking with fixing Porky's foot? Though I have my doubts about whether we can save it.'

She'd do everything within her power to keep from amputating if it was up to her. Everything and then some. Porky deserved that. And so did she. Here was an opportunity to fly, show what she was made of, and she wasn't going to blow it.

Having showered to remove the grit and now dressed in theatre scrubs, Sam entered the small, crowded operating room, desperate to know how his sergeant was getting on, fearful of the answer. That foot hadn't been in good shape. Porky was a professional soldier who prided himself on being the fittest, and was one of the best at what he did. Without his left foot he'd be relegated to an office out the back of nowhere for the rest of his army career. He'd hate that with a vengeance.

Jock looked up as the door shut behind him, and tilted his head in Madison's direction, his eyes wide. Was he telling Sam he was impressed with their new medic? Or things had gone badly for Porky? No, he knew Jock and didn't think he was telling him something was wrong.

Moving closer to the operating table, he saw Madison was leading the surgery. So Jock had handed the reins over. Interesting. That meant she knew her stuff. Jock was a perfectionist who let no one rain on his parade.

Maddy worked with infinite patience, putting that decimated foot back together. Out in the desert Porky's foot had looked done for. Now there was a strong chance it'd be hanging around for a long time to come. *Go, Maddy.*

'Watch an expert at work. Never seen anything like it, considering she's not an orthopaedic surgeon.' That was awe in Jock's voice.

'Seems Madison doesn't do anything by halves.'

'Worked out on patrol, then?' Jock hadn't taken his eyes off the surgery still going on.

'Couldn't fault her. Got a sharp pair of eyes on her, too.' She'd been the first to see that kid crawling towards them. She'd also kept her promise to not let dust whirls disturb her. There had been a couple of instances when her hand had touched her midriff but her focus had been fixed on their environment, observing everything around them.

'The guys okay about her?'

Sam nodded. Oh, yeah. They more than liked Captain Hunter. She could've asked them to crawl backwards all the way to camp and they'd have leapt at the chance to win her attention. 'She slipped into her role as easily as a cold beer could slide down my throat right about now.' Madison hadn't tried to show she knew what to do, had instead got on with the job as required. Not every officer arriving out here for the first time behaved like that.

When he stepped closer to the operating table Madison raised her eyes. 'Didn't hear you come in. Thought you'd be hours away still,' she murmured, before returning her attention to the job in hand.

He was already forgotten. Porky was in very good hands. His eyes dropped to the operation site. Her long, slim fingers moved deftly, gently, even though Porky wouldn't be feeling a thing. Ideas of what those fingers might feel like on his own feverish skin wound around Sam, teasing him, lifting goose bumps on his arms. Her movements were smooth, purposeful. The suture needle caught the light as she pulled and pushed it, reminding him of one of those spinning rides at the fair. Now you see it, now you don't. Now I touch you, now I don't. Damn it.

Jamming his hands on his hips, he stared down at the patch of floor between his feet. Nothing there to distract him or make him curl his toes.

*Get me a cold drink, fast. I need to drown these crazy thoughts before they take hold and wreck my common sense for ever.*

Except this was nothing new. He'd felt the same tightening, same need warming his blood whenever he was interested in an attractive woman. Often. But today—today's longing was about more. As though the whole package was a possibility.

'You clear that police site?' Jock's sharp question interrupted his daydream.

'Without a hitch.' He risked watching Madison some more. 'Porky's got a good chance of a reasonable recovery, then?' he asked no one in particular. Singling out Maddy would make her more important in his eyes, and he so didn't want to do that. He'd gone too far along that track already.

Again she glanced up to him, like she was connected to him somehow. That could prove awkward considering where his mind had been headed. 'No guarantees on how well the foot will function but I think we can say he's going to keep it.' There was a challenge in her eyes, telling him not to argue the point.

He wouldn't. The sergeant needed all the positive vibes he could get. 'That's a better prognosis than I gave him two hours ago.'

'Me, too,' Madison conceded. 'I didn't think he stood a chance, especially when Jock asked me to take over.'

That hit him smack bang in the chest. She'd admitted she might not have been the best person to do the job without a thought to the consequences for her own reputation. Again that annoying question sprang into his mind. *What's happened to you?* She got spooked by dust whirls, admitted she wasn't perfect when it came to operating, had accepted he'd been in charge on that morning's patrol without a murmur. His gaze dropped to her midriff, or where it should be under the loose scrubs she wore.

*I so don't know you. But I sure as hell want to.*

'Sam, did you find what got Porky?' Jock asked as the operation was being finished. 'Madison thought he might've stepped on a landmine but I reckoned he'd have lost a lot more than his boot if he had.'

'There was nothing left of the explosive device to investigate but we found a homemade pressure bomb on the other side of the building that we're presuming was the same as what Porky trod on. Small, amateurish but still destructive.' It'd been pure luck the second incendiary device hadn't been completely buried so that the sun's rays had caught it enough for Cop to investigate. Someone else could've been badly injured if he hadn't.

'Porky, Cop. What's with all these nicknames?' Madison asked. 'How come you haven't got one, Jock?'

Sam and Jock laughed.

'You have? Jock's a nickname?'

'The man's a Scotsman from way back,' Sam told her.

'Three generations ago,' Jock growled. 'Nothing Scottish about me.'

'He likes haggis.' Sam shuddered. 'How anyone can eat that is beyond me.'

'You got a name, Sam?' Madison asked as she straightened up and dropped the suture needle into a dish. Her hands immediately went to rub her lower back.

Heat clawed up his cheeks. 'Ah, no.'

'Rooster.' Jock laughed.

Her eyebrows rose endearingly, a query blinking out of those large eyes. 'Do tell.'

'Cock of the roost,' Jock happily explained.

Madison laughed, a pure, tinkling sound that went all the way down to his toes, heating bits of him on the way past.

He loved that laugh. It touched the chill inside him, taunted him, spoke of life and love. Swallow. No. Haul on the brakes. This had to stop. Now.

'What shall we call Madison?' Jock asked. 'You remember anything from your school days?'

As those dark blonde eyebrows rose in surprise, Sam shuddered. *I need to get out of here.*

*Now.* 'Maddy,' Sam replied, careful to avoid anything contentious as he headed for the door. The muscles in his back tensed, his skin prickled. He could feel her eyes boring into the back of his skull.

'That's not a nickname.'

He had to stop his getaway and deal with this, otherwise Jock would keep at him. 'I can't think of anything else,' he lied. Inferno would get her more attention than she already had. Besides, he was the one feeling like an inferno, she was merely the match.

Jock asked, 'What about your family? Did they have a pet name for you?'

She was smiling when she said, 'Spark. As in bright spark.' Instantly the smile disappeared, replaced by anguish. 'But not now.' Her hand went to her stomach, rubbed lightly, left then right. Did she even know she did that? Did she realise the brown shade of her eyes turned muddy when she was disturbed? And how her forehead creased, bringing those shaped brows closer together?

'Maddy it is,' he said quietly, hoping to dispel her distress, hating to see Maddy terrified at unguarded moments. Looking around, he knew he wouldn't find the cause in this room, that it came from somewhere deep inside her, but he looked anyway. Preferring to think Madison was all right, that nothing bothered her so badly she went still and pale in an instant. Knew he was lying to himself, but what was a guy supposed to do? Go hug her? Whisper sweet nothings in her ear until she laughed? He'd get an elbow in the gut for sure.

Would she survive out here where nothing was guaranteed? Not her safety, her sanity or her privacy.

More than anything, he wished for that. He needed to know she'd be okay, would survive the coming months without another wound to her soul.

But only time would take care of her. Time, her colleagues and her own strength. He'd have to wait long, agonising months to be sure she made it safely back home.

And when she did, he couldn't be there to welcome her.

## CHAPTER FIVE

'THAT QUEUE ISN'T getting any shorter,' Madison muttered as she wiped her forehead with the back of her hand for the umpteenth time.

'I wonder why.' Sam grinned.

'You think it's funny?' The line of soldiers waiting to see a doctor was ridiculous. 'Don't they have anything better to do? I mean, they're very fit. You can't tell me every one of those men is ailing from something.' None of the soldiers who'd presented to her had actually been sick or in need of any treatment, so what was going on here?

'I'd say there's nothing wrong with most of the men.' Sam's grin only widened. 'But there hasn't been a new, good-looking female come on the base for months now.'

These guys were lining up in the heat and dust to get a look at her? 'Get out of here.'

'No way,' he answered with a wink, apparently deliberately misinterpreting her. 'I deserve the break since I've been working my butt off dealing with non-existent aches and pains when not one patient...' he flicked fingers in the air '...actually wanted to see me. I don't have the right curves.'

No, but he had all the muscles any woman could wish for and they appeared to be in excellent working order. Of course, she couldn't comment on *all* of them. 'Right. I'll fix this.' She strode through the door. 'That's it, guys. Show's over. Get back to work and start being useful.' Or whatever they were supposed to do at the end of the day.

A private stepped up. 'I've got a pain in my belly.'

Madison read his name tag. 'How long have you had this pain, Private Johanson?'

'It started while we were out on patrol this morning. Thought I'd eaten something off for breakfast and it'd go away after a time, but it hasn't.'

'Where exactly in your abdomen is this pain?'

'All over the place.' The soldier ran his hand lightly over his belly.

Maddy wondered if she was being stitched up yet again, but something about the guy's demeanour suggested maybe not. 'Come in and get up on the bed.'

Relief lessened the stress in his face. 'Boots off?'

'No, but pull your shirt up.' As she gently felt his abdomen he lay dead still, not even breathing. She pressed deeper, feeling for any sign of a distressed appendix.

'That's not nice,' the private groaned. Sweat popped on his brow and upper lip. Impossible to fake that.

Her fingers continued gently probing his abdomen.

He sucked air through clenched teeth.

This man had a genuine complaint. 'That was worse when I lifted my hand away?'

He nodded.

Another indicator she was on the right track. 'Where did the pain start?'

With a groan he hovered his hand above his

right side near where she'd applied light pressure. 'About here. Stayed there for hours then spread around.'

She checked his name badge again. 'Reece, I'm going to take your temperature and then a blood sample.'

'Thanks, Captain. What's my problem?'

'You might have appendicitis.'

'Great.' Reece closed his eyes.

Once she had an EDTA blood sample Madison made a smear to stain when it had dried, then ran the blood through a very basic haematology analyser. 'Slightly elevated WBC,' she told Sam when he came across to see what she had.

'Checked the smear for immature neutrophils?' he asked.

'Will as soon as the slide's stained.' Neutrophils were the white cells that reacted to infections and in this case if the numbers were increased and/or immature the result would back her diagnosis. 'Twelve percent band forms,' she told Sam ten minutes later. A textbook result for appendicitis.

'Our man's going to Theatre, then.' He headed

for the exit. 'Back in a moment. Going to get our anaesthetist out of the mess. I'll assist you.'

Madison shook her head after him. Still checking up on her. It should irk her, but it didn't. Probably because she was exhausted and would be glad of another pair of eyes on the job. Hard to believe she'd arrived only thirty hours ago. So much had happened she'd believe anyone who told her it'd been a week.

'Private, I'm going to operate to remove your appendix. The good news is I don't believe it has perforated.'

'Glad you've got something terrific to tell me, Captain.'

'Hey, I'm sure it's scary, Reece, but this is a straightforward operation. You'll be sitting up drinking tea and eating a sandwich before you know it. Have you heard of keyhole surgery?'

'Sounds small.'

'Exactly. You won't even have a scar to show off.' Why some men liked to flaunt their wounds was beyond her. Guess a surgical one wasn't hideous like burns. Most scars didn't turn people into paranoid nutcases like she'd become. While explaining what she was going to do in basic terms without the ick factor, she undid the laces of Reece's boots and pulled them off. 'Might as well get you comfortable. When did you last eat?'

'At thirteen hundred hours. Didn't feel much like food so only had a snack bar.'

He hadn't been in her patrol so must've been with Jock. 'That's in your favour. Here's Cassy to help you get ready.'

The private blushed. 'Hi, Cassy.'

'Reece.' Cassy looked anywhere but at their patient.

'Let's get this happening.' Sam strolled into the room. 'Anders is on his way. Just finishing dinner.'

'Lucky guy,' Madison muttered. Lunch seemed days ago.

'Here.' Sam passed her a chocolate bar. 'Get that into you.'

'Thanks.' She tore off the wrapper and took a bite. Rolling her eyes, she said, 'Heaven.'

'It's not a good look when the surgeon faints halfway through an op.' Sam gave her one of those smiles she already treasured. They were warm and encompassing, aimed straight for her heart, whereas his grins were fun and wicked and she liked those, too.

'You have a point.' Crazy but she found herself constantly looking out for those smiles. They made her feel as though she wasn't on her own. Not that she was, being surrounded by military personnel, but there were times when she needed someone beside her that understood where she came from, who she was. *Hey, that's not Sam. He doesn't have a clue about me.* But they had walked the same streets, attended the same school, followed the same career paths.

Another bite of the treat he'd brought her. The chocolate gave her an instant boost. As did a glance at Sam. Or maybe the sudden energy rise was the result of his smile. Whichever, her shoulders lifted and her blood warmed, and the tiredness dogging her took a hike. A temporary fix but that was all she needed to get through the next thirty minutes.

'I see I'm not rostered on in here tomorrow morning.'

'Never say that.' Sam shook his head at her. 'You're only tempting fate. There's no such thing as not being on duty around here.'

'So I've noticed.' Madison didn't try to dampen the warmth cruising her body, waking her up.

*Watch it. Don't let him do this. He'll be gone in less than a week and I don't want to be left wondering how well we could've got along.*

'You going to stand there daydreaming all night?' the man winding through her veins asked. 'How about getting a move on so we can hit the canteen sooner than later.'

'Yes, sir.'

'Watch it,' he retorted, as he nudged open the door into the scrubs room. 'We're not on patrol now.'

'No, but you'll be keeping just as close an eye on me throughout the operation.' The warmth was cooling. She was no longer a registrar. Appendectomies were straightforward surgical procedures. Sure, things could, and occasionally did, go wrong, but she was more than competent.

'Don't panic, Madison. I'm not checking your operating abilities. You're a qualified surgeon with a ton of experience behind you. I'm sure you've done numerous appendectomies. I'm simply assisting as I'm on duty and ready for something more exciting than torn nails or pretend sore throats.'

She'd got that wrong, then. 'You know my medical career history?' She wasn't sure how she felt about that.

'Just supposing, having been there myself,' he muttered over his shoulder. 'Med school, specialty training, and then deciding what to do next. Except I'm still surprised you're not working to becoming established in private practice.'

'So am I,' Madison replied without thought. Yikes. Now he'd ask again why she'd changed her mind, and she wasn't about to talk about the year she'd had away from medicine while she'd got her health back. She needed a diversion and quickly, judging by the questions brewing in his eyes. 'I don't remember you being at our school in years nine and ten.'

He named a low decile establishment on the outskirts of the city. 'I moved across town from there to live with Ma and Pa Creighton in year eleven. It was a bit of a shock starting in with your lot. For one, my grades were appreciated, not poked fun at.'

'Are the Creightons relatives? Distant ones?' It wasn't usual for strangers to take a child into their lives like that.

'No.' Water splashed over the side of the basin when Sam shoved the tap on full. Whatever he said was lost in the noise of running water and the harsh scrubbing of his hands.

Now she'd gone and stirred up things apparently best left alone. Placing her hand lightly on his shoulder, she tried to ignore the ripple of muscles under her palm. 'I'm sorry if I've overstepped the mark.'

Under her palm Sam went rigid. The scrubbing stopped and he stared down at the floor, his arms braced each side of the basin. 'Ma Creighton and my mother were friends when they were kids. When Mum got a cleaning job at the same school Ma Creighton taught at they renewed their friendship.' Lifting his head, Sam locked his gaze on her. 'Mum died and the Creighton family didn't hesitate to take me in. I could've kept going across town to my old school but I'd hated it there, was glad of the opportunity to start afresh.' Hurt dripped off his words.

He'd started in a new school and a new family all at once. Lost his mother as well. That explained his take-me-or-leave-me grins. He wanted to be liked but was afraid to risk himself. 'Must've been hard for you. Did you have any close friends who knew?'

His headshake was abrupt. 'No. I liked it that way.'

'I get it.' She really did. Sharing her anguish was not happening. She didn't want sympathy, just honest friendship.

'See you in Theatre,' Sam muttered as he pushed past her.

'Sure.' Madison followed, her mind absorbing this information. He must've been so lonely at times.

Something he'd obviously been an expert at covering up.

'Glad that's over,' Madison commented around a yawn. 'Reece came through easily enough.' The top half of her scrubs hit the laundry basket. One hand firmly held her T-shirt in place to stop it riding up and revealing her scarring, something she'd become practised at when around other people. Using communal showers when she'd first joined the army had been awkward, and had seen her getting to the shower block very early or equally late in order to save her pride. A towel had always been on hand to wrap around her body if someone came in. Once a group of younger female officers had deliberately gate-crashed her ablutions but after seeing her fully naked they'd apologised and left her alone from then on. The real surprise from that experience had been that she'd never heard a word about it around camp. It was enough for her to forgive the women.

'No reason why he shouldn't have. He's fit and healthy.' Sam's scrubs followed hers. 'Let's see what the cook's got for us.'

'I'll give that a miss. I'm not hungry.' Who knew where her appetite had gone but the thought of food made her nauseous.

'That chocolate bar wasn't enough,' Sam muttered.

*No, but spending any more time with you would be too much.* 'Probably not.' Another yawn. 'But sleep's more important right now.' There was cotton wool in her skull and grit in her eyes, and tomorrow she had to be on her mettle for whatever came her way.

'You reckon you'll nod off now? Right after doing an op? On an empty stomach?' Disbelief radiated out at her from deceptively calm eyes.

Sam knew she wanted to avoid him.

He wouldn't understand she was doing this so she didn't get too invested in him. So that when he left her heart would be fine. Hearing that snippet about his mother's death and the Creightons' generosity had her wanting to dig deeper into who he was. Which was a slippery slide down into trouble. She'd stay clear of him as much as possible.

That's how it had to be. With Sam and any man who interested her. *Really?* Her heart slowed as sadness clogged her blood. Really. She was not exposing herself, her body, to be laughed at or, worse, turned away from with horror. Anyway, the fact she mightn't be able to have children would be another turn-off for most men, and one she wasn't strong enough to face.

'Hello, Maddy, anyone home?' Sam waved a hand in front of her eyes.

'No, I'm asleep on my feet,' she retorted. Slapping her hands on her hips, she took her confusion out on him by growling, 'Quit hassling me, Sam, before I do something I regret.'

'This I can't wait to see.'

She poked his chest with a finger, bounced on her toes. 'I'm exhausted, but I'm also feeling wired.' Energiser bunny in disguise.

'In other words, overtired.'

'Thank you, Doctor.' Throughout her body muscles tensed, ready for action of some kind. Any kind.

An annoyingly big smile hit her in slap bang in the stomach, winding her up so fast it wasn't funny. At the same time her insides resembled melted jelly and all her tension evaporated. How did he do that? She, of all people, knew better than to be taken in. Not just by Sam, but by anybody. Yet… Her thigh stung where her palm landed hard. Sam smiling at her just—just got to her in ways no one had for a long time. Make that in ways she hadn't allowed for a long time, ways she'd fought hard to remain immune to. And tonight she had no fight left, was exhausted beyond measure. Spinning around, she aimed for the door. 'See you tomorrow.'

Sam followed her outside as though nothing bothered him, like he wanted her company. 'Come for a walk around the perimeter.'

That's what she was about to do. Alone. 'You go and eat. You must be hungry.'

*Get away from me, give me space to douse the warmth you've created so that jelly sensation can solidify back into concrete.*

'You're jumping off the walls from an adrenalin rush brought on by operating.' His hand on her elbow did nothing to cool her down. Quite the opposite.

'As I already said, yes, Doctor.'

His hand remained on her elbow. He matched his strides to hers. 'Throw in exhaustion and you're more than hyper. A fast walk will help quieten you down. Followed by food, you'll then sleep the sleep of the dead.'

Madison jerked away from him. 'That's taking things too far.' The cooler night air was soothing on her flaming skin. Not enough to calm down and become rational again, but it was a start. Heading in the direction of the perimeter, she began striding out fast, her chest rising and falling rapidly.

Sam stuck by her side. 'Glad you're seeing things my way.'

'I don't need a chaperon.'

'I could do with stretching my legs, too.'

For the first few minutes Madison said nothing, her fists beating the air as she jabbed them up, jerked them down, up, down. Dust lifted at every step she stomped. Her skin was soon hot and sticky. 'This is stupid,' she huffed through a dry mouth.

'You don't like silence?' So light and chatty. Nothing was rattling the man.

So she tried a different tack. 'Did you always want to be a doctor?'

'No. That came after the fireman craze at six,

a cop driving fast cars at ten. I finally thought being a doctor would be cool when I was fourteen.'

She huffed a lighter breath. So far so good. 'Find me a small boy who hasn't wanted to do those things.'

'Who said I was small?' he quipped. 'What about you? A princess, a dancing queen, then a doctor?'

Because there was no insult in his tone she let him off with his quip about being a princess. 'Just as predictable. A vet, as many of the girls in our science class wanted to be.'

'What happened? You'd have easily gotten into vet school. Top girl of our year, and all that.'

He remembered? Wow. 'Vet school's hard to get into, and the end of many students' dreams. When I told Dad I wanted to be a vet he made me get a job at the SPCA at the weekends and at a vet clinic cleaning cages after school. Said I needed to learn vets weren't all about cute puppies and kittens but dealing with their pain and suffering.'

'A wise man, your dad.'

'Yep. I couldn't handle it when any dogs came in injured. Their pain was my pain, in an over-the-top teenage kind of way. As Dad had known, that made me realise I couldn't do the job. Those dogs, and the cats, at the SPCA would look at me with their big, trusting eyes, as I got them ready to visit the vet. Sometimes they didn't come back. I always felt as though it was my fault if they were euthanased because I'd been the one to prepare them for their visit.'

'You don't feel the same about humans?' Sympathetic amusement crackled between them.

'Of course I do, but it's different. Don't ask me how, it just is.' She'd fallen to bits when her dog had had to be put down after being hit by a car. She'd refused to replace him. She could still drag up a mental picture of Buster's big trustful eyes on her as she and her father had taken him to the vet. 'I don't have to put down my patients.'

'No regrets?'

Madison shook her head. 'Not at all. I like helping people as much as I adored attending to those animals. Being a surgeon suits me, although it is quite intimate in a way.'

'The invasiveness of it?' Sam nodded. 'I'm always awestruck by how people who know nothing about me are willing to trust me enough to operate on them.' They'd reached the mess block. 'Ready for something to eat?'

'I'm still not hungry.' But that hyper feeling had quietened down. 'Think I'll head for my barracks.'

'Have a drink with me and we can share a plate of fries.' He held open the door leading inside the mess.

'Do you always boss everyone around like this?' she asked as she slipped past him into the bright light of the nearly empty mess, her stomach winning over the need to put distance between them.

'Only people who beat me at physics.'

'Did I?' Laughing, she sat down on a stool at the bar and said, 'Why did you go to Auckland to do your training? Were you running away from Christchurch?'

# CHAPTER SIX

YES, IN ONE way Sam had been running away. 'I won a scholarship to Auckland University.' He still filled with pride at his achievement. 'I was determined to go to med school and a scholarship made it a lot easier.' The money he'd made filling shelves in the local supermarket after school hadn't exactly been overwhelming. Moving to Auckland hadn't been cheap but there had been no shadows lurking in dark corners, no memories of his mother at the local shops or in the library there.

'Why medicine?'

Ah. More back story coming up. He wasn't used to talking about his past, or anything close to him, come to that, but it seemed he couldn't help himself around this woman. At least he'd soon be out of there and not likely to bump into her again. 'Mum was chronically ill for as long back as I can remember. She was a diabetic, an asthmatic, and had Crohn's disease. Living in poverty didn't help her situation.'

'That's so unfair, copping all those illnesses.' The sympathy in Madison's voice could undo him if he wasn't careful.

Now he recalled why he never talked about this stuff. But he'd started, couldn't seem to stop. 'When I was old enough to understand that Mum couldn't get out of bed some days because of her health and not because she was the lazy cow my father called her, I tried to do everything possible to help her. It wasn't much.'

'You were only a kid. It was your father's responsibility to care for her, surely?'

'You've got to be there to do that. He left when I was four. Just upped and walked away one day after the beer ran out and Mum couldn't find the energy to drag herself to the liquor outlet to get him some more.'

'Oh, Sam. You got a bad deal.'

He glugged down some of his water. 'Yes. And no. We were dirt poor but I was always sure of Mum's love. She struggled to hold down a job because of her health and that made me feel bad because I knew she only went to work to give me things.'

'She was a good mum.'

When Maddy's hand covered his, Sam struggled to hold back the sudden tears welling up. Damn her, he did not need this. He hadn't cried for his mother since her funeral. But seemed that now he'd started he wanted to talk about the rest. 'It wasn't until she went to work at that school and hooked up with Ma Creighton again that she stayed in the same job for more than a year. I suspect Ma Creighton stuck up for her whenever the school board talked of getting rid of her.'

'Friendships can be the best thing out.' Her hand tightened on his.

He didn't want friendship with Madison. She'd want more of him than he was prepared to give. Pulling his hand away, he continued, now in a hurry to finish his story. 'From the day Ma and Pa Creighton took me in and made their home mine I was determined never to give them any reason to regret their generosity. They were exceptional, kind and considerate, and at the same time they never went soft on me.'

Yet, except for a couple of brief phone calls, he hadn't spoken to them in a long time. All part of his withdrawal from being too near to anyone. People he got close to tended to desert him one way or another and he couldn't risk losing the two who'd stepped up for him when he'd been a confused and angry teen. Guilt waved at him again, cramped his gut. He missed them so much, thought of them most days. Next week, he knew, he should finally visit them.

'You want another of those?' Madison tapped his water bottle.

Letting him off the hook? Had she sensed his pain, known to back off? 'I'll get it.' He should walk away from her while he still could. But it was nigh on impossible when Maddy managed to wind him up and soften his stance all at the same time. During the past day and a bit he'd thought more about his future, and his past, and Madison, than he had in two years. It was as if she'd taken a chisel to those tight bands around his heart and created a gap through which his real emotions were escaping. Emotions such as need, want, love, and—dared he admit it?—excitement. He couldn't afford to give in to these feelings. Another shiver; deeper this time. It had been too long since he'd believed there might be someone special for him out there. The risk was huge, but right this moment it was hard to deny himself a glimmer of hope. Seesawing between two worlds, he swung towards Madison, went with keeping the conversation light and chatty. 'I did have a blast in Auckland.'

'Has the city recovered?' she asked with that cheeky glint he enjoyed more than a cold shower on a hot day.

Though a cold shower might soon be necessary to cool the heat banking up internally as he watched her shift her curvy backside on the stool, unconsciously letting off fireworks in his belly, further lightening the weight wedged there since she'd turned up on his patch. 'I hope so.'

Sam tilted forward, halving the gap between them. Her scent floated on the air, instantly transporting him back to the peach tree in the yard of the only home he'd had with his mother *and* father. Large, ripe, succulent peaches. It had been the year he'd turned four and he'd spent hours under that tree in summer, playing in the dirt, shaking the branches to bring down the fruit to shove in his mouth and feed his hungry belly, sticky juice sliding down his face. Dad used to sit there, reading the paper, smoking, drinking beer, pushing a toy truck around when he could be bothered. At the end of summer his dad was gone, out of his life for ever.

Sam jerked back. *Stop this nonsense.* He didn't do thinking about the man who'd fathered him and then discarded him easier than last week's bread.

When he next looked at Madison he found her deep gaze fixed on him, almost as if she was searching for something he wasn't sure he wanted found. She sure had him thinking about things he'd long buried. Another diversion was needed. 'What about you? You stayed on in Christchurch?'

'Yep. I'm close to my family and my girlfriends went to Christchurch University as well.'

'Why the army?' Never had he asked so many questions of someone. What was in the water?

'To get away for a while. Decide what to do with my career. And to do something for my country. I like that we can help other people less fortunate through the military.'

'Tell me to shut up if you don't want any more questions, but did your failed marriage have anything to do with leaving Christchurch?'

'Shut up, Sam.' It was said without anger. Without any emotion at all. She was hurting. He could see it in the white fingers gripping her bottle, in the flat line of her mouth, the dull eyes.

He backed off instantly. 'Fair enough.'

Then she paid him back with, 'You never married?'

'Not even close.' A shortage of women hadn't been the problem. Finding one he could fall in love with had been. Then William had happened and he'd understood he wasn't entitled to happiness.

Madison was eyeing him with caution. 'So no little Sam Lowes running around?'

'Nope. I wouldn't dream of having children if I wasn't in a happy, strong marriage.'

Her mouth twisted up in a wry smile. 'I have to agree.' Then she chuckled. 'My sister has four kids. She married an Italian and they live just down the road from our parents.' Maddy's face lit up. 'Those girls are gorgeous. Little minxes, every one of them.'

'Four kids is a handful.'

'Yeah, but what a problem to have.' She smiled, big and deep, and touched something inside him. Then her expression became wistful, probably thinking of the kids she might've had if her marriage hadn't gone off the rails.

'Not for me.' An image of Madison holding her own baby, smiling softly, rocking gently, her face full of love, wove through his mind, wouldn't let go. It was a beautiful picture that he needed to burn. His hand jerked, his knuckles banging against his glass and upending it. Water pooled on the counter and dripped over the edge. Snatching up a cloth to mop up the mess, he was reeling, his head spinning. Damn but Madison tripped him up too easily just by being normal.

Madison was wiping her fatigues where water had soaked the fabric. 'You don't want four kids?' Her dazzling smile faded as she looked directly at him. She knew something wasn't right.

'Hard to imagine when I'm here.' Which reminded him—where was their food? As good an excuse as any to escape while he got his brain back under control. 'I'll see what's cooking in the kitchen.'

So Madison adored children and from the look that had come over her when talking about them would be quite happy to have a brood of her own. She'd make a great mum. Probably be quite strict but soft as butter on the inside.

After ordering fries and chicken, he plonked an elbow on the counter and leaned back to study Madison. She was chatting to the barman, no longer wary of his questions and what she might reveal about herself. He'd swear she'd told him more than she'd intended to. But, then, his usual reticence had taken a hike, too. It showed Maddy was capable of tipping his world sideways. What it didn't show was why. Why her? How had she been able to sneak under his radar even a tiny bit when that had been iron cast?

Look at her. There was part of his answer. Guys were gathering around Maddy, eager to tell her about themselves, to claim her attention, drawn in by that face that could launch a thousand ships, the body that promised heaven, and the smile that would not let them look away. He completely understood their reaction; she'd captivated him within minutes of turning up on his patch.

Crossing over to the group, he reached around one officer for his drink and was astonished to hear Madison say, 'Make way for Sam. That's his spot.'

Pleasure oozed through him like he'd been handed a present to unwrap. His fingers curled around the icy bottle of water she nodded to, and he nudged a guy off his stool. 'Thanks, mate.'

Madison's lips were pressing down hard on a burgeoning smile as she tapped her bottle against his. 'To Kiwis in out-of-the way places.'

He tapped back. 'To unusual places.' Playing it safe? Damn right.

'What do we do around here on our days off?' Maddy asked no one in particular.

'Go into town to check out the stalls at the markets.'

Her face lit up. 'Markets? Bring them on. I can't think of a better way to spend a morning.'

'Happy to show you around any time,' one of the guys told her.

*I'll drive you into town whenever you ask.* Sam swallowed hard. *Down, boy. Be the mature man you pride yourself on being.*

'Here you go, Captains.' Two plates of steaming food were banged down on the counter between Sam and Maddy.

'Thanks, Bud.' His mouth watered as the wonderful smell of fried chicken reached his nostrils. 'Get stuck into that.' He pushed a plate closer to Madison and glared around at the crowd. 'Give us some space, guys.' *I want to talk to Captain Hunter—alone.*

Surprisingly the officers did back off, heading to the snooker table.

'This is yum.' Madison munched on a drumstick.

'Unhealthy and delicious,' he agreed as he reached for some fries. 'For someone who wasn't hungry, you're making short work of this.'

'I never turn down a good offer.'

His chicken went down his throat only half-chewed as his mind came up with more than one good offer. At least he managed to keep them to himself. Just. 'What was all that about the dust yesterday?'

Her plate hit the counter with a thud, quickly followed by fierce colour staining her cheeks. Her breasts rose on a long breath. She was pulling on a shield. 'I told you. I thought it was smoke,' she ground out in a don't-ask-me-any-more tone, bringing his focus back to where it should be.

'What happened, Maddy?' Why the fear of smoke? Or was it the fire that had caused the smoke that had given her grief? Had she lost her possessions or a place she frequented because of fire?

Madison slid off the stool she'd been sitting on. Her eyelids were blinking rapidly, as if he was shining a torch in her eyes to see beyond her reticence. She was keeping tears at bay, or hiding them from him.

Neither made him happy. 'Talk to me, Maddy. Please.' Though it was none of his business, he wanted to know everything, had to wipe away that despair, that agony darkening, dulling her eyes to the colour of burned wood.

She'd turned for the exit but came back. Her hands were fists at her sides, her feet wide apart, her chin pushed forward. But she wasn't fooling him. Regret had replaced the pain in her eyes. 'I don't know you well enough, Sam.' She spoke softly, carefully, and her words wrapped around him, tugged him in.

Would she biff him around the head if he enveloped her in a hug? He shrugged. If that's what it took to banish whatever was bugging her, tying her into knots so tight she might take a week to loosen up, it would be worth it. But— 'Try me.'

'I don't think so.'

'Tell me why.'

This protectiveness had started yesterday almost immediately after that dust had got to her. Then on patrol in the morning he'd been constantly alert, watching out for her—and keeping his attention hidden. Madison was beating at his long-held barricades that kept people exactly where he wanted them. He should be the one rushing out of here, not Madison. But he couldn't, wouldn't. 'You're not trusting me?'

'Bang on, Sam.' Blink, blink.

'Why not?' Her response didn't hurt. He understood from his own perspective. But he would like different from her.

Sadness mingled with despair as her eyes locked on him. 'Would telling you it's none of your business work?'

He shrugged deliberately. The next move was hers.

'Okay, then how's this? I don't talk to anyone about what happened to me. Get it? I trust no one not to hurt me.' Her hand fluttered over her stomach. It didn't touch down, just hovered in a protective way. Or was that as a reminder of something she needed to fear? 'I'm sorry.' She turned on her heel and left him.

'Maybe you should,' Sam whispered to her fleeing back. The muscles in his legs corded, his knuckles on the hand holding his drumstick whitened as he struggled to remain on his stool. He had to let her walk away, drop whatever was upsetting her, because she'd asked him to. Because he wasn't the right person to share her pain.

Clink. The water bottle banged his bottom teeth as he took a swig. The cool liquid wetted his parched tongue and slowly the tension eased. *I've missed something important.* It was staring him in the face and yet he could not grasp it.

Madison didn't laugh freely often, and when she had moments ago that sound had been full of everything but happiness and amusement. She didn't rush to get onside with everyone around her. That lack of trust had a lot to answer for, but what had brought it on? What had gone down to make her so wary? There was a broken marriage in her background. Was that the root of her problems? But the way she subconsciously touched her midriff when upset suggested the question might be what had hurt her, not who.

Smoke. Fire. That touching movement she made. She'd been in a fire. Was that the complete answer? No way of knowing, but there had to be more. Sam stared sightlessly in front of him as the questions nagged. This guessing game was a waste of time with no substantive answers available.

# CHAPTER SEVEN

'HOW'RE YOU FEELING this morning, Reece?' Madison read the chart from overnight. 'Everything's looking good.'

'Fighting fit, Captain.' It was said with a chuckle. 'Captain Lowe says I can go on patrol this morning.'

Sam was here already? And she'd thought she was early, skipping breakfast in the hope of avoiding him for a little longer. Last night's revelations on her part had been a little too close for comfort and she wasn't ready to see that understanding in his eyes again. 'Is that so?'

'Just kidding, Captain.'

'I believe Captain Lowe is taking a patrol out to that old police building again. I'll see that you're fixed to join them.'

The private's face dropped. 'If you say so, Captain.'

Madison laughed. 'Just kidding, Private. Have you had breakfast?'

'Yes. Though not enough. Could do with some more bacon and eggs.'

'I bet you could.' She headed for the door, calling over her shoulder, 'That's a no from me.'

'What are you saying no to?' Sam stood in front of her, hands in pockets, a smile tugging at the corners of his mouth.

'Reece wants a second breakfast.' The way the top of Sam's fatigues moulded to his chest, defining that amazing shape, had her nipples in tingling peaks. He looked good enough to eat. She was hungry after all. But suddenly not for toast.

'You look like you could eat two as well.'

Rolling her head from side to side, she tried to negate the cravings swamping her. 'I'm fine,' she muttered.

*Let me out of here before I touch him, run my hands over that divine body.*

'You haven't eaten.'

*Didn't say I had, but I want to.*

Sam hadn't finished. 'You finished your run at six hundred hours, less than thirty minutes ago.

Time only for a shower and to tidy your room, wouldn't you agree, Captain?'

*More than enough time to try out that body,* Captain. Voices came from behind her, snapping her out of her wishful thinking. 'You had nothing better to do than see who was out on the track this morning?'

'I was finishing my run as you began yours.'

Which meant he'd been outside some time around four a.m. 'Trouble sleeping, Sam?'

'About as much as you. If I'm not mistaken, your lights were on at that hour.'

He wasn't mistaken. But he might not know they'd been on for hours before that. 'I was messaging home.' And beating up the pillow, guzzling water, pacing the ten strides from wall to wall over and over. And thinking about Sam. Mostly thinking about him. She might've left him in the mess last night but his questions had followed her into her room and right into the short sleep she'd managed before waking up completely around two. Those blasted questions had still been there, coated in the husky tones of Sam's voice. Rough, sexy, annoying, caring. Yeah, that about summed him up.

'Go to breakfast, Madison. You're not putting in a full day without eating properly. The heat is debilitating without starving yourself.'

She huffed at him. 'You're not my keeper. If I'm not hungry then I'm not hungry.' Even to her that sounded petulant. But the thought of food had nausea rising up to the back of her throat, while the lack of sleep made her feel like something the dog had chewed and left on the side of the road. 'I don't always have breakfast, okay?' she added for good measure, because she knew she was wrong to go without food.

It didn't work. 'Out here you do. We never know what's going down from one hour to the next and we have to be prepared. That means having regular meals.' His hands were on his hips now, his fingers pressing deep as he leaned towards her. *'Comprendo?'*

Very nice hips. Shaped the perfect body outline. His torso was all muscle. Basically he was a lean machine. The youthful softness she vaguely remembered had gone from his face, replaced

with lines and knowledge. A fighting man, prepared for battle, as all the soldiers on base were.
As she was. And if she had to go into battle—
please make that a skirmish—she needed to be
fully ready. Which meant breakfast. 'You win.'
She turned away, intent on getting back here as
quickly as possible.

'Madison,' Sam called after her.

*Ignore him.* She paused, faced him. 'Sam.' Her
heart went wild, beating a rhythm all of its own,
not one she recognised. But, then, she wasn't
at all familiar with the reactions that pelted her
body whenever Sam was around. Phew, but it
was hot in here.

He stood in the doorway, his hands back in his
pockets in that, oh, so nonchalant manner of his.
Which meant he was about to say something she
mightn't like. 'I wasn't trying to score points off
you, merely looking out for you.'

*Knock me over. Did I hear that right?* Did she
like that? Oh, yeah. She did. Lots. She melted,
a slow sensation of warmth trickling through
her belly, over her skin, encompassing her heart.
With this man at her back she didn't have to

worry about a thing. But the days were running out and soon she'd be back to looking out for herself. Dipping her chin, she acknowledged, 'See you in a bit.' He didn't need to know how his statement made her feel, but she could enjoy the warmth that molten sensation brought.

'Don't take too long. I hear there's already a queue forming to see the new doctor.' He flicked her a grin before heading away. He'd got the last word in. Again.

She didn't care. Especially when he grinned in a sexy way that stirred up all sorts of sensations in places she really should keep under lock and key. The man was almost too good to be true. But she was never going to find out how good he was. Hot as— Yeah, so was the air around here. And her blood. Phew. The back of her hand slid across her forehead. How had she not noticed all this before?

There was only one way to control herself. Remember Jason and how he'd switched off from her the moment he'd seen her scars. Sure, he'd hung around for six months before asking for a divorce, but during that time he'd slept in the spare room—so as not to disturb her sleep apparently—and he'd never held her close or kissed her, or said he loved her. It had taken one look at her body for him to leave her mentally.

Madison chewed toast thoughtfully. She could not afford to forget that lesson. Not even for an hour of bliss.

'Eggs sunny side up.' The cook slid a plate in front of her.

'Ta muchly,' she said. Her stomach was in turmoil now. Could it handle eggs on top of that little shock she'd given it? But she did need to eat. Sam had been right about that.

Sam. Sam this, Sam that. Her second full day here had barely started and already he was taking over every thought process.

Hurrying through her eggs and coffee—which did stay in place—she returned to the medical block. A few hours working alongside the man would soon have her brain back in sync. He'd annoy her to bits and she'd be thinking what a pain in the butt he was. *Not what a gorgeous sexy man he was, one she'd like to take to her bed and learn more about?*

Shut up, brain.

*Wasn't your brain talking, it was your hormones.*

Thank goodness for long queues of bored soldiers needing vaccination updates. The hours flew past without Sam getting under Madison's feet too often. 'What's on after lunch?' she asked him as they wrapped up the morning.

'The commander's letting some of the locals in for us to treat. They'll be brought across in batches of four or five, depending on who the patient is and who's with them.'

'As in children and their parents?' Woo-hoo, she was going to see people who needed more from her than all the morning's soldiers put together had. 'What can we expect?'

'I'll tell you after you've eaten lunch.' She couldn't tell from his poker face if he was joking or warning that the afternoon wasn't going to be pleasant.

She'd go for the joke, and hope she was right. 'That good, huh?'

'You're not always easy to wind up.' Sam laughed.

A deep-bellied sound that curled her toes, and had her trying to think up things to say just to evoke more laughter. Nothing came to mind. 'I used to be. Guess I've changed.'

The laughter died in his eyes. 'People do, Maddy.' Somehow he'd moved right up to her without appearing to shift. And now his hand was on her chin, his thumb softly caressing her jawline, back and forth, oh, so gently. *Don't stop.* 'I think it's called life.'

He didn't know the half of it. Couldn't. Not unless he'd emailed someone back home, and that was unlikely. From what she'd learned these past few days, if Sam wanted to know something he asked outright. Anyway, who would he ask about her? He hadn't kept in touch with anyone she knew.

'So I've heard,' she choked around a huge dollop of lust. That, unusually, was the stronger of the emotions roiling through her. Sam's thumb was magic, eliciting all sorts of sensations to spread out from her chin. She was leaning towards him, against his hand, afraid he'd stop.

Maddy took a big step backwards, disappointment rising as Sam's hand slid away. If he had her in such a twist from a mere thumb rub, what would…? *Don't go there. You're never going to find out. Understand?* Oh, yeah, she understood all right. One look in the mirror at her abdomen would give her all the brakes she needed and more. Unless she made a blindfold for him. A sharp laugh huffed across her lips, bitter in its taste. Sam really had got to her if she was coming up with such ridiculous ideas. 'Right, lunch.' She strode away without looking at him, for fear of melting on the spot.

'I want to kiss Maddy.' Sam could not drag his eyes away from her as she crossed the parade ground, heading for the mess. That butt was doing manoeuvres in her fatigues that had nothing to do with soldiering. Moves that had his hormones in a spin.

'I'd wait until lights are out,' Jock drawled from somewhere behind him.

Sam swore. *Did I speak aloud?* Take that as yes. 'Shut up, Jock.'

'Just saying.' He nodded. 'You going to tell Maddy what you just told the whole medic unit?'

'What?' Sam scanned the room. They were alone.

'You're running out of days to make good on your wish.'

'That's got to be a plus.' Kissing Maddy would not be wise. Getting all wound up in knots of need would only make for a very uncomfortable flight back home. Not that there'd be any kissing. She wasn't going to allow him close enough. Besides, he wouldn't be able to stop at that. And he had to. No. He had to stop this daydreaming before acting on it. Not after.

Jock rubbed his belly. 'Let's go eat, man. We've got a fair whack of patients this afternoon and you know how frustrating that's going to be.'

*Wrong word, buddy. I'm frustrated already, and it has nothing to do with patients.*

'What made the boss agree to letting more people in today? It's not like we haven't fulfilled our quota for the week.'

The commander stuck to the rules when it came to allowing locals onto the base, even those with serious medical conditions. Something both Sam and Jock disagreed with. Helping those in need was integral with being doctors, but try explaining that to the commander and they'd find themselves doing more patrols than usual. The commander was the guy who'd take the fallout if anything went wrong, though.

'No idea, and I'm not asking. He's just as likely to change his mind.'

'True.' Sam sure as hell didn't want those cute little kids missing out on treatment because he'd said something out of order. 'Wonder how Maddy will cope with the clinic?'

'You really have to ask that?'

'No.' Just making conversation. Of course her name had popped up unbidden. It seemed nothing he did banished her from his mind. She hadn't crept in. She'd bashed her way into his mind, his dreams, his body. A groan escaped him. 'Four days to go.' And counting. Could he get beyond them without following through on the driving need turning him in an ever-decreasing circle? Without dealing to the almost over-whelming need to kiss her?

Only time would answer that one. Four days and counting.

'They don't cry when I touch their broken arms or infected sores.' Madison was in shock. She'd seen children as young as two this afternoon and their stoic little faces had cut into her heart, making her want to wrap them up and take them home.

'It has you wondering what else they've en-dured, doesn't it?' Sam held up an X-ray taken of a six-year-old boy's arm Madison had handed him. 'Both the ulna and radius are broken. Looks like blunt force trauma to me.'

'His mother said he fell off the roof of their dwelling.'

'His mother? Or the interpreter?' Sam shrugged. 'Remember, what's most important is getting those bones set and on their way to mending. It's all we can do.'

'You're right.' But she didn't have to like it. 'You want a hand putting a cast on?'

'Come and work your charm while I try not to hurt the poor little blighter.' Sam nodded. 'We'll give him something for the pain first. Can't stand to inflict any more than he's already dealing with.'

Straightening those bones before applying a cast was going to be awful for the lad. And for them. 'I think he's underweight for his age, but I'm not sure what's normal here.'

'He very well could be. Any fever, cough, breathlessness?'

'Not that I've noticed.' And she would've. She'd done all the obs, and more. The boy had barely stirred as she'd poked and prodded as gently as possible. The only sign he was in distress was his big black eyes getting larger.

'Let's get this over so the wee guy can go home with his mum.'

'How did they get here?' She hadn't seen any vehicles outside the camp since she'd arrived.

'They walked.' Sam held up his hand in a stop sign. 'Don't even say it. We are not allowed to give them a lift back to town, but sometimes it so happens a truck needs to go for some supplies just as people are trudging away from seeing us.'

'Cool.' Madison picked up the equipment to make a cast and followed Sam over to their patient, who lay curled up beside his mum. 'We have to give Khalid an injection,' she told the interpreter.

When the boy heard that from the interpreter he pushed harder against his mother but didn't utter a sound. 'I'll try not to hurt you,' Madison said in as soothing a voice as she could manage. Rubbing Khalid's arm with her palm, she felt him tense, so continued to rub until he slowly relaxed. When she finally slid the needle into his muscle he didn't blink, but who knew if that was because he hadn't felt the prick or not.

Sam opened the top drawer of a cabinet by the bed. 'Here you go, young man. A lollipop for being so brave.'

The small mouth slowly expanded into a smile as Khalid snatched his treasure from Sam's fingers. His mother said something and the boy nodded at Sam.

'I'm picking that's thank you in Khalid-speak.'

Sam grinned briefly before working quickly to align the radius at the break.

'Right, now for the messy bit.' Madison spread a plastic cover over the bed and began to apply the cast. She wanted to work fast so Khalid would soon be out of his misery, but she also didn't want to make the cast too tight or too loose, so he'd have to come back for a second attempt. 'I can't remember the last time I did one of these.'

'Back to basics, isn't it?'

'Yes, and you know what? I'm enjoying it.' Sometimes it was easy to forget the simple stuff, hand it over to a nurse and move on to the next surgery.

Sam said, 'I've been watching you. You've enjoyed helping these people.'

'I have.'

'Don't get too involved, Maddy. They're not why we're here. You've got to remember that. If you don't you could find yourself in a dangerous position one day. Not everyone is as they seem out here.'

*Go and spoil the moment, why don't you? Even if you are right.*

For a moment there she'd forgotten the military side of being here, had become lost in the medical world that was her first love. Swallowing the flare of annoyance his words had caused, she acquiesced. 'You warned me of that the day I arrived.'

'Think of Porky and his foot. That's why we're here. Not to get blown up but to defend the innocent. As an aside, we do what we can for the locals if time and safety permit.' Serious Sam was as mesmerising as the other versions. Then his face softened and he totally had her attention. 'I don't ever want to hear that you've been injured while here, Maddy.'

Moisture filled her eyes. That had to be the nicest, kindest thing anyone had said to her in a long time. Her family had learned to keep those thoughts to themselves after she'd broken down one day saying they were undermining her efforts to be strong and capable alone. That had hurt them but since then they'd all tried hard to follow her wishes. Now, after a simple comment from Sam, nearly a stranger, she understood she'd been wrong. 'I'll be doing my damnedest to keep anyone, especially my family, from hearing any such news.' Suddenly she missed her mum and dad, her sister and those nieces so much her arms ached to hold them and her heart slowed with sadness.

'You'd better.' Sam's voice had become gruff, deeper and darker, full of an emotion she didn't recognise. Maybe he cared more about what happened to people than he'd admit.

'Sam?'

'Better get on with the last patient.' He quickly turned to snatch up a piece of paper from the nearest desk and headed to a man and his son, waiting quietly.

Sam was in a right old pickle. That page he'd grabbed was the score sheet from last night's medics' snooker contest, not notes about any patient. Maddy chuckled. Sam in a stew was like a small boy trying to decide which flavour ice cream he was going to have.

Downing his water, Sam nodded to the sergeant behind the bar. 'Another thanks, Randy.' No such thing as drinking too much water out here.

At long last the day was over, and unless, touch wood, there were any incidents during the night, he was free to do as he pleased. That did not include kissing Maddy, something that was becoming a bit of an obsession since the idea had first struck. No, he needed to find another way of letting his hair down and eliminating the pent-up needs keeping him on tenterhooks since he'd gone and told Madison he'd be worrying about her.

'Up to some rock?' Jock leaned a hip against the bar.

'Exactly what I need.' An hour getting lost in the guitar with the band would knock him into mental shape. 'Boyse and Carter around somewhere?' The drummer and xylophonist were integral to their band.

Jock, the voice and other guitarist, nodded. 'They're on their way over.'

'Show time, then.' Sam stood up. Friday nights in the officers' mess were his favourite. He'd play his guitar and try to get lost in the music, something not always possible since the quality of music depended on who was stationed on base at the time. There'd been some clangers in the past all right but tonight he'd have no trouble getting immersed in the music.

As he settled on a stool and picked at the guitar strings, tightening two, he glanced across to the corner of the room where a group had gathered with Madison in the centre. Of course. Not that she looked overly comfortable, wasn't putting on the charm or being too friendly with any of the men. When she glanced his way and met his gaze she nodded and gave him a knowing smile.

Knowing what? Racking his brain didn't toss up any ideas of what that had been about.

'You joining us?' Jock nudged him.

'Try and stop me.' For the next half-hour Sam played whatever tune the other band members started, letting himself go in the rhythms of rock music. His mind was blank apart from the keys he played, the strings he strummed and picked. The music flowed over him, eased the tension he'd been carrying since Madison's arrival on base.

Ah, Madison. Snap. The tension was back. He scanned the room. There. Parked on a stool, a soda in one hand, her feet tapping in time to the music, and a smile of pure happiness lightening her face. For the first time she appeared to have no worries in the world. Then she looked his way and stood up with a determined expression and placed her drink on the counter.

Now he remembered. 'Hide the microphones.' Last year at school. The senior's social, Maddy and her pals on stage.

'She can't sing?' Jock asked into the silence that came with the end of their current song.

Her voice had been strong, alluring, sweet, but having her up here beside him…? Not happening.

'She doesn't know a C scale from a fish scale.' *Don't drop a bomb on me tomorrow for lying.* If Maddy picked up a microphone he was leaving. One guitar down wouldn't matter, the other guys could make great music without his input, while having her standing beside him, belting out words in a voice made for an angel, would stir him up even more. Wouldn't matter if she was in tune or not.

'Let's do something heavier,' Jock said, and started banging out another rock song.

Maddy's face lit up some more, and that smile would now blind a city with its intensity. Her feet were done with tapping; now she was moving on the spot, her hips swaying and her arms moving above her head in time to the music.

Sam needed a drink—fast. His tongue was stuck to the roof of his mouth, his throat so dry he couldn't even squawk along with Boyse's singing. Just as well. The guys would fire him on the spot.

'Get that down your throat.' A can appeared in his line of vision.

He nodded thanks to Jock. Still couldn't talk. How was it his mate seemed to know what was going on in his head almost as soon as he did? Damn but that cold liquid was good. Wet in the right places, cooled the heat in his throat, even tasted wonderful. Did absolutely nothing to chill down the heat tightening his groin.

'Can I join in?' Madison stood in front of him, that supple body the only thing his eyes could see.

Of course he nodded agreement; of course he did. Damn it.

Boyse called out the next song, and began the beat. Not a tune Sam had been expecting, but with a bit of luck it would be beyond Maddy. She'd sung the light girl band music that got everyone up dancing. He began playing his guitar, refusing to watch as she stepped between the guys to stand legs wide, head back and a microphone to her mouth. He did not see her lips almost swallow the mouthpiece. He did not feel apprehension and awe alternatively cool and heat his skin. No, not at all.

And then the first words came out of her mouth and Sam forgot to play, forgot where he was, forgot everything but Madison.

So much for thinking she couldn't sing rock. She *was* rock. She owned the song, took it from ordinary to sensational. She moved with it, became it, striding, swaying, dancing from one edge of the band to the other and back again, her head tipped so far back it seemed impossible she wouldn't crash into something or someone.

Where was her long hair when he needed it to be hanging behind her?

He knew his mouth had fallen open and his eyes were wide, felt his lungs stall, his stomach sit still in shock, and the beat of his heart was so out of whack with the song it was awful.

What happened to sweet? What was spilling out of Maddy's mouth was raw emotion. Deep, husky notes that played his senses like a bow on violin strings, that lifted goose bumps on his skin and sent prickles of heat down his spine. This was nothing like her speaking voice. She'd stepped into the song as though she'd experienced what was behind the words. Maybe she had. Maybe they'd hit on the one song she could relate to so deeply.

And then— And then she took it up a level. Sam's gut tightened. Where did that come from? The drama behind the words filled the air, stopped everyone except the band in their tracks, drinks frozen in hands on tables or halfway to mouths. Sam's guitar rested on his thighs, his fingers slack against the strings. He was beyond playing, had lost the ability to pick a tune.

This was not a one off—Madison would sing every song as though she'd lived it.

As she proved again and again over the next thirty minutes. She had the room mesmerised. The guy behind the counter was out of a job while she sang. Sam reckoned every male fell in love with her during those loud, emotional, magical minutes.

But not him. Of course not. Somehow he finally managed to play his guitar, keep in tune and not look like a three-year-old with a plastic toy. Somehow he didn't give Jock an elbow when he cocked a knowing eye at him and said, 'If that's not knowing her scales, what is it?'

Sam didn't have an answer. What could he say that wouldn't dig a bigger hole for him to fall into?

Four days and counting.

# CHAPTER EIGHT

MADDY WAS BUZZING. Joining the guys for a few songs had been a blast. She hadn't sung as though there was nothing else in the world but the message in the song for a long time.

Come on. That's not how she'd sung at all. Neither had she ever before. Tonight she'd poured every painful emotion possessing her into each word and note. The fire that had destroyed everything good about her life had strangled her with deeper, harsher emotions. Tonight she hadn't been able to stop them expanding through her. But at least she'd faced them, hadn't run away.

And she was buzzing. How did that work? Because she still carried the agony of losing her granddad, the anger at Jason's rejection, still bore the sadness of not knowing if she'd have a child one day. The big unknown.

Like she was drugged or something, the buzz

did not fade as she recalled the infections that had run rampant through most of her body as her burns had seemed to take for ever to heal. Chest infections, kidney issues and stomach problems from the endless antibiotics she'd swallowed. But the worst by far—a tubal infection that had refused to clear up for months. No one had been able to state categorically whether infertility would be a result. According to the gynaecologist there was only one way she'd find out for certain, and the woman hadn't sounded very positive. Another mark against her already uncertain future. Something else she couldn't ask a man to accept.

Madison refused to let the familiar desolation shove her high away. Tonight had been good for her. She'd let a lot of pain go during that short span of time where she'd poured everything into the songs and forgotten where she was. Right now she was on top of the world. She would probably crash tomorrow but tonight she'd enjoy the ride. It was the first in a very long time.

Reaching for her water bottle, she glanced around the noisy room. Laughter and jokes were coming in every direction from the officers she was starting to get to know. No sign of Sam, though.

The band had set their instruments aside to take a few drinks on board and he'd been the first to the barman to grab a water bottle, but now he was nowhere in sight.

The buzz faded a little. She wanted to share it with Sam, not these people who didn't understand her. Sam understood her? Since when? Yes, she thought he did, at least a little bit, because of the grief she'd noted in his eyes when he'd let his guard down.

'He went outside.' Jock stood beside her.

She looked into the understanding gaze locked on her and whispered, 'Thanks.' But what if Sam didn't want to talk to her? Why should he? 'Maybe I'll wait and see if he returns.'

Jock tilted his head at her. 'Yellow doesn't suit you.' He said it quietly, calmly, not menacingly or cheekily. Just a nudge in the right direction according to Jock.

She slid off her stool, tightened her grip on her soda bottle and said, 'Thanks again.'

Her skin squeezed tight in the cooler outdoor air, and for a moment she couldn't see beyond the line of light thrown from the open door. As her sight returned to normal she looked around. No sign of Sam. But he'd be out there. It was where he went when he wanted to be alone. *So go hunt him down.*

He was walking, head down, hands stuffed in pockets, covering the track that followed the perimeter with a slowness that seemed foreign to the man she was getting to know. So far she'd only seen a guy who tackled things without looking over his shoulder.

Madison hesitated, familiar doubts nodding at her. 'Yellow doesn't suit you.'

*Yes, thanks, Jock, got that message, but what if Sam tells me to go to hell, to get out of his face?* She'd do as he demanded. But she didn't want that. They had started something over the last few days; a friendship based on next to nothing but one she was grabbing with both hands. A friendship with someone who was unaware of her history, had no compunction about asking the hard questions because he didn't understand the ground he was treading on. It had been a long time since anyone had treated her without first pulling on kid gloves. Other than the army, of course. The military didn't care about things like that, only demanded loyalty, hard work, and obedience. A balm for her prickly nature. And now Sam seemed to be approaching her from a different perspective to either of those. An approach she liked, appreciated, wanted more of. She felt there might be a cure for her in there.

*So, take a deep breath and go talk to the man.* Or walk in silence with him. Whatever. But do something. He won't mind. He'll walk away. He'll… She stepped after him.

'Maddy, thought you'd be lapping up the crowd's attention for a while yet.'

If he thought that'd turn her around he was wrong. She kept walking towards him. 'It was fun.'

'But?'

*I'd like to be with you.* 'Why aren't you inside with your band buddies?' When his mouth tightened, she swore under her breath. She'd just flipped the question back at him. 'Let me start again. It was more than fun. Singing with you and the guys was incredible, and I loved every moment. I'd forgotten what it's like to let rip without thought of anything else.'

'How many years since you last sang to an audience?'

Madison got the feeling he was really asking what had made her stop. 'Too many.' Had he seen through her usual façade?

She had thrown herself into the music, put everything out there for the first time ever. Could be because she was so far from home, from where her nightmare had begun. Whatever the reason, it had been liberating, and she yearned to be able to tell someone—Sam?—about her insecurities. *I'm trapped until I do.* Madison gasped. That was true. Until tonight she hadn't seen that. Already, coming to the Peninsula was proving to be good for her.

But standing here with Sam, already the shutters were closing. When he said, 'Tell me more,' she swayed on her feet, like she rocked on the edge of a precipice, tightening her muscles around the pain and anger, wishing the words would escape across her tongue.

She took the easy option in answering his question; the tried-and-true one, the safe one. The only one she trusted. 'You know what it was like. When I was studying and doing long shifts as part of my training, there wasn't any time for much else.' Only Jason, and he'd put the kibosh on her singing, saying it belonged in the shower, if at all. She gasped. He *had* been a bit of a control freak, come to think of it. 'Guess I just forgot to sing.'

'That's a waste.'

'Thanks. I wouldn't win one of those TV singing shows.' She didn't hit every note perfectly, lost her way in the tune sometimes.

'Maybe not, but you'd get a standing ovation. When did you start singing rock? I mean—' he was shaking his head with something resembling disbelief '—your voice is ideally suited for that genre. It's so expressive. Unbelievable.'

Her lungs swelled up, her heart stretched to almost bursting at his compliment. That it was genuine she was in no doubt. A step closer to him.

There was wonder in those sunny eyes. Wonder for her. And somewhere deep, deep inside her, another knot of pain, of anger and confusion, slipped loose and began to unwind. One coil at a time the tightness that had held her upright for two long years was slackening off and she wasn't falling down. There just might be a future for her that held some of the hopes she'd had when growing up. She might be able to dream again.

'Maddy.' Sam reached for her and tucked her against his chest, his arms wrapped around her.

Against her cheek she felt his lungs rising and falling faster than normal, matching her quickened rate. Under her palms, resting against his waist, muscles were tightening. Breathing deep, she savoured the mix of aftershave, sweat, man. Sam. Clutching at his shirt, she leaned back to peer up at his face, seeing the lines carved out by grief, by the determination that must've been behind him becoming a surgeon, the humour that hid his feelings, and the loyalty he had for those he cared about.

If she dropped all her defences and let him in then what? They didn't have a future together.

She didn't know him well enough to trust him with everything. He could still wreck her. But…

Sam held Madison tight against his hungry body and absorbed her into him. Her heat, softness and those curves, the surprise that had sparked at him when he'd told her what he thought of her voice, her hair tickling his chin. *This is Maddy.*

Desire rolled through him, tightened him. This is what he wanted. Now. With no thought to the consequences. Shock stunned him. He followed a rigid line when it came to friendship and relationships, never deviated, and yet here, tonight, he wasn't; couldn't haul up the usual defence mechanisms. His body was afire with need.

To hold her wasn't enough.

It was too much.

Turmoil churned his gut, fear chilled his blood. This hug had to be enough. They couldn't have a relationship, not even for one night, because he suspected that once he let his guard down with Maddy he'd never be able to pull it back in place. And he had to.

He wasn't free to fall in love and marry, not

when the guilt kept him hogtied. How could he be happy when he'd taken that from William the day he'd talked him into a final tour with the army before he married his fiancée? William hadn't been keen to delay marrying Ally for another six months, but he'd given in to Sam's plea to go to Afghanistan with him. Now Sam could not move forward, could not be happy and take enjoyment from life when William and Ally couldn't. There were many obstacles to him settling down, and they were all in his head. Didn't mean they were any less real.

Gently setting Maddy aside, he worked hard to ignore the disappointment that dulled her eyes and drooped her shoulders, mimicking what was pouring through him. He re-ran the band through his head, playing those songs that Madison had blown out of the water. That voice. It had stroked him, rasped his skin, evoked all sorts of fantasies. What if he did follow through and hauled her back against him? Oh, and kissed her? And…

'Let's walk.' Then he surprised himself. He caught up her free hand and slipped his fingers between hers.

A jolt reminiscent of an electric current he'd once copped when he'd tried to change a power switch for his mother pinged where their palms touched. *Let go of her now.* Just like when he'd been zapped for real, he couldn't. Beggar for punishment that he was, he wound his fingers tighter around Maddy's. And she reciprocated. Which meant what?

Stretching his steps into strides, he took them out to the perimeter and beyond the mess and bar, away from prying eyes. Unable to drop her hand, he enjoyed the sheer delight of holding hands with a woman. *This woman.* Warmth worked its way up his arm and down into his chest, softening his breathing, turning his fears and guilt into a puddle of wonder. And worry. This was not how things were meant to be for him now. Madison. Stick to Madison and this whole wanting her thing might evaporate in a cloud of reality. *If only.*

So what now?

Letting go of her hand wasn't an option.

Maddy couldn't believe it. Holding hands with Sam was so—so out there. It wasn't even high-powered, hot, sexy stuff. It was gentle and caring and nice—she hated that word but it was true. All right, try wonderful. Unbelievable, more like. Perfect. Yes.

She squeezed his hand to make sure she wasn't making this up. His fingers tightened briefly around hers. Definitely for real.

Had to be the heat and the foreign location and that music and... Madison sighed, long and slow. Had to be something in the drinking water because holding hands was nothing like what she'd expect with this man. He gave the impression of being more the let's-get-in-the-sack-fast kind of guy. Exactly what she felt around him when she admitted her feelings. Don't go there. Enjoy the moment. Because it would only be a moment, a few minutes at most, then Sam would realise what he was doing and drop her hand like a hot potato. And one of them needed to be sensible.

If she talked, would that burst the bubble? But her blood was fizzing, her whole body buzzing from earlier and now topped up with a dose of Sam. Holding hands was nowhere near enough. His mouth on hers would go a lot further towards improving the situation.

Madison gasped. Again kissing was on her mind. What would he do if she turned to him and placed her lips on his? Would he kiss her back? Soft and gentle? Hard and demanding, giving as much as he took, she'd bet.

'You okay?' her biggest distraction asked.

'Fine.' If wanting to kiss him was fine. If needing to get closer was fine.

'Damn.'

'What's wrong?'

'You and me. That's what.' Was that longing making his voice lower and huskier than usual?

She was probably imagining it because of the need clawing through her. 'How are we wrong?'

'As in for each other, Maddy.' There. The way he dragged out her name, turned it into a caress, turned her insides into that molten mess of need she was learning to live with on an hourly basis.

'Maybe it's our time.' Gulp. She'd given herself away with that desire-laden comment. A beggar on her knees couldn't be more obvious.

Sam extricated his hand.

She'd gone too far. But he was here, for real, and every stop sign had disappeared.

'I'll tell you something for nothing, Madison. When you were singing that first song the emotion that poured out of you, I've never heard anything like it. You had me in the palm of your hand. You could've done anything to me at that moment.'

She'd sing it again—now. Definitely begging. 'If only I'd known.' She tried for a laugh, came out with a squeak.

Sam managed better with a chuckle that didn't sound strangled. 'I'm glad you didn't. I could've ended up looking foolish in front of the guys.'

'And that matters?'

He turned to her and with one finger lifted her chin so there was no avoiding his eyes. 'You've got to live and work with them.' There was no grin for her now. Just complete seriousness. 'We can't forget we're on different tracks. I don't do relationships, long term or otherwise, while I think that's what you're looking for.'

'Wrong. I won't be marrying again, or getting into a permanent relationship of any kind.'

'You will get over your broken marriage, Maddy. You must.'

If only it were that simple. She stumbled sideways, putting a gap between them, away from those eyes boring into her in case he saw the truth. That she wanted him despite everything. She could not let him near, would not undress in front of him, or let his hands explore her body. He'd unwittingly given her the wake-up call she needed. While she'd been leaning in for more of Sam, desperate to get close in a sexual way, yearning for his touch, to touch him, she'd completely forgotten the truth. She was not going to let him see her body. Not going to see that look of horror when it filled his eyes, twisted his mouth. It would break her completely.

She couldn't trust herself to accept someone might want her as she was. Didn't believe it possible. Not when her husband, who'd declared his undying love for her only two days before the fire, hadn't been able to accept the new her.

Sam watched the argument going on in Madison's head. It leapt through her eyes, marked her face, flattened those kiss-worthy lips. She wanted him as much as he did her. But fear had her fighting her desire all the way. Something he understood completely.

But… One kiss. What harm could that do? It wouldn't mean there was more to come, but it would satisfy an ache.

Or create a bigger one.

There was that.

One kiss would definitely crank up the heat into an inferno.

But he had to taste her. Had to know those lips, had to satisfy a quest he'd begun unknowingly only days ago. At the same time it was as though all the barriers he'd erected were tightening, warning him not to do it. But the clawing need for affection and sharing was stronger.

'I think I'll head inside.' Madison stood before him, looking sad and lost.

He did what he shouldn't. He ignored those damned warnings. 'Don't go yet.' Reaching out, he took Maddy's shaky fists into his hands and wrapped her arms around his waist. She fitted like she was an extension of him. And that scent—he drew a long breath and savoured that summer fruit memory, rearranged his memories from a four-year-old's to a man's. Nothing set his senses tripping the tango like the smell of Maddy.

Dropping his head, he found her mouth, covered those enticing lips with his, and knew her softness. Her sharp indrawn breath made him pause until she relaxed into him. Then he went back to kissing her. One hand reached up to push through the silk that was her hair. The other cupped her chin as he continued to taste her, and an all-consuming need burst alight inside him, making everything he'd known before redundant.

When her body melted into his those glorious breasts pushed against the hard muscle of his chest, her hips pressed his, while the apex of her body touched his hardness.

Sam groaned. This was hell on earth. This was wonderful.

Maddy tensed. Her hands left his waist, flattened on his chest. Slowly she lifted her mouth away from his, tipped her head back to lock those eyes on him. 'Sam?'

'Yes, Maddy, it's me.' He recaptured her mouth

before she could deny him another kiss. One had not been enough. Two wasn't going to be either.

She sank back into him, causing him to relax, except where it mattered. His tongue stroked her lips, her mouth. It wasn't enough. He tasted the skin on her jawline, and below her ear.

Under his hands he felt the change in her posture, the slow tightening of her arms before she began to pull away.

His first reaction was to haul her closer, tighten his hold, kiss her deeper. But Madison was withdrawing, and he had to allow that.

And being Madison, if he took too long to let her go, stole another kiss first, she'd probably want to kill him.

*And I want to live. Really want that more than anything.* Sam jolted backwards, his arms dropping to his sides while he rocked on his feet as though slammed by a runaway truck. *I'm starting to feel alive for the first time in years. I want to love, and laugh, and make a home, and settle down, instead of wandering wherever the army sends me.*

This was what happened when those protective ties around his soul began unwinding.

This was what happened when Madison Hunter had stepped into his life.

This was dangerous.

There was too much flotsam to deal with before he could even begin to undertake a relationship. He had to walk away from Madison, let her get on with her life without him, because he wasn't able to become a part of it. She'd been badly hurt. He could not add to her anguish. He had to hold onto that raw emotion she'd poured into her singing so as he didn't add to it.

But he was damned if he'd ever forget that kiss.

# CHAPTER NINE

'WE'RE WANTED AT the hospital in town,' Sam told Madison the moment she stepped inside the unit.

So much for last night's kiss. The way he was looking at her, it might well have been a figment of her imagination. Only problem there was that her brain wasn't that imaginative. Hadn't known that a kiss could transport her to places out of this world, or turn her inside out with desire. If that's what Sam's kisses did to her, she hated to think what his lovemaking might do. A very good reason not to go there, since this morning she was struggling to cope with acting like nothing had happened. As for sleep after she'd crawled between the sheets around midnight—forget it. Sam had ruled. In her head; had even tickled her heart.

Yet here he was, looking relaxed and cool, like nothing had occurred between them.

Her blood began to boil. Sam did that to her. *Don't let him. Be as blasé as he appears to be.* Maddy appraised him harder, finally saw the tell-tale twitch of that amazing mouth. Not so cool after all. *Yeah. Got you.* She wanted to punch the air, but refrained by folding her arms across her breasts. 'Why are we headed to the hospital and not out on patrol, as we're supposed to be?'

He tossed some packets of swabs at a bag. His casualness didn't fool her this time. The packets missed their destination. 'There's been an accident...' he flicked fingers in the air '...involving a school bus.'

'Can't the local doctors cope?'

'We're under orders, Madison. This is what we do, follow orders.' He snatched the swabs up from where they'd landed on the floor and shoved them inside the bag. 'We'll travel in convoy with armoured vehicles as there're reports of trouble at a village along the way.'

Her heart thumped against her chest. *Reality check. This is what I was sent here for, not for sensational kisses.* She was about to go out into danger. Or the possibility of it, which amounted to the same thing, according to her heart, which was now beating a sharp and rapid tattoo. 'What do you want me to do? Do we take supplies with us?'

'The truck's being loaded as we speak. You're in charge of making sure nothing important is left behind.'

In other words, she was superfluous to requirements but he was stuck with her. Digging deep, she found a smile and refused to utter anything antagonistic. Two could play at being nice. Except she meant it. 'On to it.' She reached for the check sheets that hung on a clip by the phone and drew calming breaths to quieten her heart before it threw itself into a fit. That patrol she'd gone on had only been a taster for bigger and scarier things to come.

'There are injured children, Maddy.' Sam was beside her.

Children. The innocent victims. She looked up at him, her eyes seeking his, looking for reassurance that she'd cope, that she'd do her job without breaking down. That he'd be there for her, with her, helping, encouraging. Why she needed him for that she had no idea, but if that's what it took to cope then that's how it was.

A light grip on her shoulder surprised her and told her Sam had read her concerns. 'It's hard, but we'll manage. Go check the supplies, Maddy.' This time his voice was like a caress, gentle and warm and comforting. A man of many facets.

'Will do.' She headed outside to the truck and Cassy, who was ordering soldiers to be careful as they loaded boxes of equipment. 'How are we going?'

'You'll need your weapon,' Sam told her.

'I knew that.' But in her hurry to see they had everything they required for their patients, she'd forgotten she was a soldier before she was a doctor. She would be a liability to the others if she wasn't armed and ready as they made their way into town.

Squashed into the cab of the truck between Sam and the driver, she stared around as they rolled out through the gate and along the dusty road, heading in the opposite direction from where she'd been before. Heat shimmered on the horizon, dust spewed from the vehicle in front to engulf their truck. 'So inhospitable.'

'Nothing like the green of home, is it?' Sam agreed.

'It hadn't occurred to me how lucky we are in NZ until I saw this.'

'Homesick?'

'Not at all.' She wasn't about to cry for home the moment things got rough.

'Too soon, I guess, but it will get you.' When she rolled her eyes at him, Sam shrugged. 'Find me a soldier who hasn't had periods of wanting to be back home with family when the heat's got to him or something's gone horribly wrong on patrol. Me included.' He was still surprising her with the things he came out with.

She told him, 'My sister emails every day, giving me snippets of what her kids are up to, how Mum and Dad are.' She wasn't admitting to missing them last night.

'That's good. Hopefully she'll keep the home-sickness at bay for you.' Doubt darkened his voice.

'Might make it worse. Who knows? But I'll not go looking for trouble. Right now I've got something more important to concentrate on.'

The hospital was rundown on the outside, but inside it gleamed. Medical personnel ran back and forth, looking harried, while children cried and mothers screamed for help. Police and armed personnel were making a show of being there. Utter chaos. But as Madison looked around she realised it was organised chaos. The staff knew what they were doing, which made it easy to slip into her role and ignore everything else.

'This way.' Sam took the lead after receiving directions from a gun-toting policeman. Was it only in New Zealand that cops didn't carry weapons as a norm? 'The men will bring our supplies through for us.'

Her first patient was a wee girl with the biggest brown eyes she'd encountered. Eyes filled with pain and resignation. 'Hello, sweetheart.' Madison knelt on the floor beside the mat the child lay on with a woman looking frantic with worry, presumably the girl's mother.

Watching over an injured child, depending

on strangers to tend the wounds, had to be any mother's nightmare. Terrifying and bewildering. Madison's hand slipped across her stomach. Children. What were her chances of having any? Despite what she was dealing with here, she'd give anything to raise her own.

Through an interpreter she introduced herself and learned the child's name was Nubia and that she'd been trampled when teachers had rushed off the bus.

Fortunately Nubia's head had not suffered any injury, but she had five broken ribs and the cartilage holding them had been torn. With gentle probing Madison discovered the spleen was ruptured. One arm was fractured and there were numerous abrasions on most of the girl's body.

Her heart breaking for the child, Madison explained to her mother about the surgery she'd need to remove the spleen. When tears rocked the woman Madison slipped her arms around her and held her until the storm passed. Then she went to see when and where she'd be operating.

'Join the queue,' she was told by a harassed doctor.

Sam came across. 'I've got a theatre lined up. We'll share.'

When she rocked back on her heels at the outlandish suggestion he added, 'It's how it is, Madison. Cassy and the others will work with us.' Then he took pity on her. 'It's not easy, I know, but you'll be fine.'

'Grow a backbone, huh?'

His finger brushed her cheek. 'You've got one, just needs a little straightening at the moment.'

Somehow she chuckled. Not a very strong or mirthful one, but better than a grumpy retort. 'Love your support.' And a few other things she wasn't mentioning any time soon. 'Let's go.'

Nubia's surgery was straightforward and she was soon being watched over by Cassy as she came round.

'No complications?' Sam glanced up as Madison joined him at his table.

'Not a one.' She watched Sam at work and admired his skill. No wasted movements, or any unnecessary use of the scalpel.

'This is Ra,' Sam told her. 'He was thrown through a window off the bus. Both femurs are fractured, and there's damage to his lower bowel that I'm about to repair.'

'Do you need me, or shall I find another patient?'

'I'd like a second opinion on the colon.'

After scrubbing up again and pulling on fresh gloves, she went to help Sam.

Many hours and procedures later they sat slumped around a metal table with the other members of their crew, drinking coffee and picking at sandwiches they'd brought with them from camp.

Madison sipped the coffee, not really enjoying the strong brew, which was unlike anything she'd had before. But she needed something to fire up her sluggish cells after working in the hot and cramped conditions. 'Glad that's over,' she muttered to anyone within hearing.

'You're not feeling up to singing with the band tonight, then?' Sam asked as he picked up a sandwich and opened it to scrutinise the contents.

'Haven't got the energy.' She wasn't going to sing again while Sam was still on base. Last night's gig had led to complications that she couldn't afford to repeat.

'You might not get off that easily,' Cassy said. 'The whole camp was talking about you this morning.'

That explained a few looks and nudges between soldiers she'd noted that morning in the dining mess. 'They'll get over it,' she sighed. 'Jock and Sam will be gone in a couple of days anyway.'

'All the more reason for a repeat performance tonight, only this time you're wanted out on the parade ground so we can all listen, not just the officers.'

'Thanks for nothing, Cassy.' Seemed everyone was deaf when it came to her saying she wasn't doing it. All she could hope was for the trucks to be late getting them back to base so that by the time they'd had showers and dinner everyone would've gone to their barracks. Hopefully.

But it seemed she had no say in the matter. By ten o'clock that night she was lounging in the bar with a water bottle in her hand when Jock and the gang started dragging the gear outside. 'Give us a hand, Maddy,' Jock called out.

'I'm not singing.'

'You're one of the band now. You have to help.'

'That's a yes,' Sam said from behind her.

She dropped her head and stared at her feet. It had been hard today, working with those beautiful, trusting children. Last night, pouring her soul into the songs had been cathartic. Kissing Sam afterwards hadn't been. Simple. Don't kiss the guy. Sing then leave. Looking up, she found Sam watching her with amusement written all over his gorgeous face. 'What?' she growled.

'You love it.'

A sigh whispered across her lips. 'Yeah, I do.'

'Come on, take an end of this table, will you? We can put our gear on it.'

'We haven't got any gear.' She hoisted her end up.

'We? Looks like we've got ourselves a singer, guys.'

The cheers were embarrassing. 'I'll need lots of soda.' It was hot work singing and leaping around in the tight space amongst the band. *And afterwards I will leave on my own, will not walk the perimeter. Will not kiss Sam. Will get some sleep.*

Sounded very boring. But playing safe often was.

'Did someone put out a bulletin about a party?' Sam asked Jock as he looked around the parade ground. Every soldier except those on duty had to be out there.

'Looks like it.'

Most of the guys were waiting for Madison, Sam would wager. Who could blame them? When she opened her mouth and let rip with the vocals she was something else.

Not just in the singing department either. Those kisses had stayed with him all night, kept him awake and hard. They hadn't gone away during the day while he'd operated. And they were there now, reminding him of what he would soon be walking away from. 'Let's make it our farewell bash,' he suggested to Jock.

Leaving the base was part of the deal when he'd signed up. It came with relief from getting through working in a hostile territory, and then there was the regret of leaving men he'd become friendly with. Some would go with him, heading for the same place, others would remain here for another six months. That's how the system worked. But this time he'd be leaving Madison just when they were getting to know each other. So why wasn't he pleased he was being saved from facing up to his guilt and denying himself the opportunity for happiness? Hanging around, pretending to push her away, all the time falling into confusion, was a recipe for disaster.

'You haven't heard a thing I've been saying, have you?' Jock sounded more than a little peeved with him.

'Tell me again.'

'You going to listen?'

'If you hurry up.' Sam tipped fluid down his parched throat and waited, almost patiently.

'Your eyes are already misting over with lust for Maddy. What are you going to do about her? I hope you've got her contact details stored in your phone.' Jock picked up his guitar and strummed a few chords, underlining his comments. 'I'd hate for you to let her go.'

'You're overstepping the buddy line,' Sam growled.

Jock rolled his eyes expressively. 'Don't go before you've told her why you're so cautious. I reckon you'll end up regretting it if you do.'

'Relationship counselling your thing, is it?' Regret was guaranteed. So was relief for what he'd save Maddy from.

'Hey, guys, what's our first song?' Maddy stepped into his line of sight, looking happy at the prospect of singing to those soldiers hanging around waiting for the music to begin.

Boyse called, 'I've written a list. Come take a look, Maddy. Let me know if there's any song you don't know.'

She gave Sam a wink. 'Now, there's a man who gets things done.' When she sauntered away she gave a wee wiggle of her butt.

And sent his hormones into overdrive. 'Someone dim the bloody lights.'

Jock's roar of laughter was the only reply he got.

Sam took one last slug of his water and set

the bottle aside. Time to get rocking. And if he couldn't ignore Maddy strutting her stuff in front of him, he'd enjoy every last movement she made, absorb each note she sang, and store up a load of memories to take away with him.

His pick slid across the guitar strings effortlessly and the guys immediately joined in. They had themselves a show.

Then Maddy raised her microphone to that sexy mouth and the notes began to pour out, stunning the soldiers into silence. Then some clown let rip a wolf whistle and the silence was over, with people swaying to the beat and joining in the chorus.

Sam played hard, barely letting one song finish before starting the next. He let the music filter into his soul and went with the energy being created out in front of them. And he watched Maddy as she moved from one side of their stand to the other, almost swallowing the mic as she belted out the emotion-filled words.

Words that scorched him. Words that tugged at his heart. Words she'd given new meaning to, and had him yet again wondering where all that pain and anger came from.

'I need a break,' Maddy called after nearly an hour. 'A cold drink wouldn't go amiss. My throat's drier than the desert out there.'

'Get that into you.' Sam passed over her favourite soda and savoured the moment her fingers touched his. Warm, soft temptation. He bit down on a groan, and shifted out of the way to avoid any more accidental touching. Despite sixty-odd personnel hanging around in front of them, his ability to control the need for her was hanging by a thread. Another touch of that satin-like skin and he'd have to haul her close, kiss that erotic mouth. Make himself some more images to carry home.

'You going to miss this?' Maddy followed him.

'The band? Yes.' Another step backwards. Then another, and he was tipping off the edge of their stand. As his arms windmilled and his feet hit the ground he heard Jock's annoying laugh.

'Good one, man.'

*Thanks,* buddy.

'Sam, are you okay?' Maddy was standing

where he'd been, her eyes twinkling with laughter and that mouth twitching. 'You should look where you're going.'

*You should back off and give me more space.* He leapt back onto the stand and brushed past her. Even that felt excruciating—so close and yet so far. 'Boyse, where's that song list?'

'Yes, Captain.' She flicked a salute in his direction, but the amusement had died, as he'd intended.

What he hadn't meant to happen was for the hurt turning her chocolate eyes to bog. He hated that bog colour. 'I deserve that.'

'Forget it. Let's get the band cranked up again.' She turned a shoulder to him, looked around for the other guys. 'Ready?'

'Madison,' Sam growled, and moved close so he could talk without being overheard. 'I did tell you how your voice affected me.' Had he really said she was screwing with his head? His hand slammed across his skull as frustration of every kind alternated between turning him hot and cold.

'I see.' Her mouth tipped ever so slightly upward. 'Then let's get the music cranked up again. I want to see more of you out of control.' Her forefingers made parentheses between them.

She was toying with him. 'Easy, Maddy. You have no idea what you're starting here.' Neither did he, when he thought about it. And he owed it to himself, if not Maddy, to give his thoughts and feelings due consideration. Wanting her and having her—two different outcomes. Outcome? It would be a conflagration if he followed through on the heat burning him up. Where was the next wave of cold coming from? He needed it. 'Guys, Madison's ready to start rocking again.'

Maddy leaned close and whispered, 'Are you sure you want this? I'm going to sing like you've never heard so you'll always remember these few days we've shared.'

He should've quit while he'd been running parallel with her.

# CHAPTER TEN

POUNDING ON THE door of her room dragged Madison from a rare deep sleep.

'Maddy, you in there?' Sam called.

'Go away. It's my day off,' she muttered as she tugged on cotton track pants and a long T-shirt. Opening the door, she said, 'This had better be good.'

It was. Sam was. Dressed in navy shorts and an open-necked cream shirt that contrasted perfectly with his tanned skin, here were all her forbidden dreams wrapped up in one stunning package. Her shoulder bumped against the doorframe and she kept it there to keep from dropping to the floor. To think she'd thought he was good looking. She'd been so far off the mark it was hilarious. If this was a laughing matter.

Sam was waving keys in front of her. 'We're going to the market.'

'We are?' Her eyes followed those keys. Off to the market. Off to the market.

'I've the loan of a car and you said you enjoyed shopping at stalls so here's your chance. I need to get a few knick-knacks to take home.' He grinned. 'If you need further convincing, this is my last day here. You won't get another offer like it.'

'What sort of knick-knacks?' she stalled.

'A couple of souvenirs for Ma and Pa Creighton. I am going to see them when I get home,' he added lamely.

'I'm glad. They'll be thrilled.'

'You think? After I've been avoiding them?' He winced. 'I've never been good at getting too close to people,' he admitted in a rush.

'That's sad. You're missing out on a lot,' said she who hadn't done any better in the previous couple of years.

Sam's fingers combed through his hair. 'Right from the day Ma and Pa Creighton took me in I worked hard at making them like me and at living up to their expectations with good results at school, but I always kept a bit of me back.'

The bit that was unconditional love and acceptance, she'd bet. 'Why?' Though she'd guessed the reason, she wanted to hear him tell her as a start to admitting what held him back. Not that she'd be following her own example any time soon.

'I tend to lose those who are important to me.'

Strange conversation to be having at her door but she wasn't about to stop it. 'Was there someone you got close to after your mother died?' He'd been very young when his father had left. The incomprehension of that act would've hurt a small boy deeply, and to be followed a few years later by the death of his mother must've been catastrophic for a teenager trying to make his mark on the world. But if he'd suffered another bereavement as an adult, that would be tough to accept, might make him feel like a pariah.

His eyes darkened as he stared blankly along the barracks corridor. His voice was a monotone as he recited the facts. 'My best mate. We met in the army and after I rescued him on day two from a pounding he was receiving from three thugs who had issues with soldiers we got on fa-

mously. Were always posted on the same tours
of duty, or at the same base back home. He was
a great guy.'

'Where is this friend now?' Something in his
expression told her this mate hadn't just decided
not to be friends any more. Another loss for Sam
to take on board and cope with. But talking about
his friend might ease some of the tension tightening his shoulders, his hands.

A shudder ripped through him. 'Gone.' Sam
turned to stare through the outside door, his
mind not with her.

Madison waited quietly, giving him space, feeling for him and knowing there were no words to
lighten his grief.

Finally he glanced over at her, hope warring
with regret in his face. 'So, you up to helping me
buy souvenirs?'

'Give me thirty minutes.' There was no way
she wasn't going with him now.

'Too easy, Maddy.' That grin was back, lopsided and uneasy but back. 'Meet me over at the
gate.' And he was gone.

She wasted precious minutes watching him

stride across the parade ground. In coming to the Peninsula she'd met a man she could relate to. A man who was sad and lonely, and yet brave and determined to carry on despite the burden he carried. He was good at disguise, hid his true self behind a cheeky grin and cocky attitude.

Inside her room, Madison looked over at her skimpy collection of mufti clothes and quickly decided on the knee-length blue shorts and white T-shirt. Then she remembered the warnings about what to wear when going out amongst the locals. Cotton pants replaced the shorts, a long-sleeved shirt the T. Snatching up a towel, she raced to the shower stalls.

As cool water blasted her from the shower head another thought slammed her. Sam had effectively told her they were never going to get close. As if that was likely anyway, with her hang-ups about her body and being left by the man who'd professed to love her, and with Sam's fear of people leaving him. What a great mix that'd make for any relationship.

She'd barely discussed her feelings for Sam with herself, wasn't sure about anything except keeping herself safe, and now, if it all got too much and she did try to explain to Sam—well, now she had the perfect excuse to keep quiet. There'd be no happy endings for them.

Sudden panic filled Madison. Sam was leaving tomorrow. They'd barely got started on getting to know each other. But it was best that way. There was no future in spending more time with him and falling a little bit in love with him.

Shampoo stung her eyes. Sluicing it away, she came to a decision. She'd spend the day with Sam, enjoy his company and have some fun. Tomorrow she'd say goodbye and accept that none of this mattered.

She'd worked with him over the previous few days, now she'd play with him. Then they'd get on with their lives and maybe, since their career paths were similar, bump into each other occasionally over the years and swap notes on what they were up to.

Her body slumped. So not what she wanted, but all she could face since she didn't have the courage to expose herself to him, or ask him to take a chance on not having a family. Besides, minutes ago he'd warned her off getting involved, and if showing him the result of that fire wasn't getting involved, nothing was.

'Try this.' Sam held out the kebab that he'd bought from the street stall in the bustling town they'd arrived in twenty minutes ago. 'It makes a good breakfast.'

Madison shook her head at him as she chewed on a mouthful of beef shawarma. The pita bread and its fillings were delectable, putting her in food heaven. Swallowing, she said, 'No, thanks. I'm not sharing this.'

'Typical.' He laughed before taking her elbow to lead them along the street towards a long, low building where a constant stream of people, locals and tourists, was coming and going. 'This is the market,' he said unnecessarily.

'The noise level's off the scale,' she muttered five minutes later, and had to shout it again when Sam stared blankly at her.

'It sure is. Try to stick with me, okay? It's too easy to lose each other in here.'

'I reckon.' She didn't want to find herself alone,

facing some the men who were eying her up and down. Tossing her sandwich wrapper in a bin, she slipped her arm through Sam's and held on. For safety reasons, of course, nothing to do with enjoying the warmth of his skin under her fingers or the sensation of belonging that enveloped her. Where that came from she wasn't sure and had no intention of exploring the answers that were popping up in her head. Not now, at least. Today was purely for fun, nothing else.

'What do you want to look at?' Sam asked.

'Those scarves look pretty.' She nodded at the stall they were approaching. 'They'd be great gifts for Mum and Maggie.' She wouldn't mind a couple for herself either.

'Ma Creighton might like one, too.' Sam choked back a laugh after some harsh bargaining had gone down between her and the stall-holder. 'Do you really need nine? How many sisters have you got?' Sam's laughter faded. 'It's strange. I feel I should know more about you than I actually do.'

'I've only got one.'

'I thought that's what you said, but seeing all those scarves I figured I'd misheard.'

'They're vibrant and colourful. My sister's going to love them, whether she wants to or not,' she retorted. 'She's four years older than me, which she believes makes her wiser, something I disagree on.'

'Sounds like I've got something in common with your sister. Disagreeing with you.' That laugh was back, nudging aside the tightness that had started creeping into her system when he'd turned it off.

'There are some similarities when I think about it. She's driven, always right, and never slows down for anyone else.' Maddy said it all with a smile and sighed with relief when Sam didn't get uptight.

'A top-notch character, then. What does she do?' His hand was back on her elbow, holding her close to his body as he navigated them through the throngs of people too busy peering at all the merchandise to look where they were going.

'She has a double degree in business studies and clothing design, which I have to admit she's exceptional at. Her fashion label is building a reputation for quality and style so fast I only hope she can keep up, considering those four gorgeous girls who keep her busy, too.'

'Bet they miss their aunt.'

'Their aunt misses them heaps.' Madison looked along the stalls for something to send home to them. 'What are you going to get Pa Creighton?' she asked next. 'We could go back for more scarves later.'

The hours disappeared in a haze of shopping, teasing, and laughter. It was the fun she'd hoped for, and more. They got along with no hiccups, like this was something they did often. The heat had built up all morning, the sun beating down on the street and the rooves of the buildings they entered.

Finally Madison said, 'I could kill for a cold drink.' She wouldn't acknowledge the heat from a different source that also drained her of energy. Heat she'd like to do something about, but then she'd spoil the day. Sam would have them back at base quick smart if he thought she wanted to get closer, get beyond kissing and clothes.

*Beyond clothes?* her brain screeched. *Seriously?* Of course not.

'I know just the place.' Sam swung some of her shopping bags in front of her. 'It's near the car so we can dump these first.'

Going back to base might be wise. With his hand on her arm for most of the morning, Sam had cranked up her desire level to a simmer. If this was what one hand could do then she couldn't imagine what it would be like to have Sam's total concentration. Boiling wouldn't begin to describe it.

'Here's the car.'

'I'd never have found it again,' she admitted as she stepped around him, putting a gap between them as she placed her shopping in the boot.

'We'll cut through that alley by the barber's. There's a café at the other end that's primarily used by Westerners, and serves hot and cold drinks.'

Sam's arm was draped over her shoulder, drawing her along with him. All she had to do was stop, tell him she wanted to go back, and that would be it. Easy. End a perfect day. But a little devil zipped her mouth shut and lifted her feet one after the other so she was moving with Sam.

The alley was dark and cold after the sun. She shivered, peered around, shivered again. 'This is creepy.'

'We'll be fine. It's not in the tourists' brochures as a place to visit or shop in, that's all.'

She upped her pace, and was glad Sam followed suit. 'Everyone's staring at us,' she murmured. The few stallholders had stopped talking and were standing watching as she and Sam headed for the far end. Two men ducked into a doorway. 'I'm not liking this.'

Sam's hand tightened on her shoulder, and she was tucked closer to his hard body. 'We're fine, I promise.'

Great. Her strides lengthened and Sam went with the flow, heading for the splash of sunlight at the far end of the alley. Then they were out in the glaring light and her heart rate started slowing back to normal.

'In here.' Sam pushed open the door and she stepped into a cool room filled with small tables and chairs. A man lounged against a counter, talking to the waiter or possibly the cook, who was rubbing the countertop with a cloth as though he had all day to do it.

There was nothing uncomfortable about the place. It was so normal Madison had to pinch herself to make sure she hadn't imagined the previous minute outside. 'Did that happen? Was I wrong to think there was something bad out there?'

'You're not used to being an object of intrigue by strangers in a foreign setting.' He placed money on the counter. 'Two sodas, thanks, Bix. Okay if we have a booth at the back?'

'Go for it.' The barman answered in a light American twang.

'Why do we want a booth?' Maddy asked. 'I'm quite happy sitting in here.' She liked the sense of space and being able to see what, if anything, was going on. That alley had spooked her more than it should have.

'Sure. No problem. Want something to eat as well?' Sam asked. 'Falafels? A kofta?'

Until then she hadn't thought she was hungry again, but the thought of those delicacies made her mouth water. 'I'm glad you haven't run out of good ideas yet.'

When the cook headed out to the kitchen to start preparing their order, the other customer downed his drink and stood up. 'See ya,' he called, and headed for the door.

Madison raised her glass and tapped it against Sam's. 'Thanks for a great day. I'm glad you brought me. I'm not sure how I'd feel about coming into town on my own.'

'Best you don't, being female and—'

*Boom.* An explosion ripped through the building, followed by another. One moment Maddy was sitting on a chair, the next she was sprawled on the floor, being rained on by ceiling tiles and cups and glasses from where the counter used to be. 'Sam,' she screeched, but heard nothing above the throbbing in her ears. 'Where are you? Sam,' she yelled as fear spread through her.

*Knew there was something evil out in that alley. We shouldn't have come in here.*

Then she heard timber creaking, followed by a loud thud, and the floor shook. More debris poured down over her. The fear intensified, tightened her stomach, chest, mouth. Not again. Please, no. She screamed. 'Sam.'

Peering through the thick dust, she couldn't find him. Her heart was blocking her throat, making breathing impossible. 'Sam. Where are you? Don't do this to me.' Was that squeaky sound really her voice? The power for the lights must've been taken out because it was semi-dark in here, making everything feel close and looming. What just happened? 'Sam, please.'

*You'd better be all right. I can't deal with something happening to you on top of all this. I don't want another Granddad scenario.*

A chill settled over her.

'Maddy.' A hand gripped her ankle. 'I'm here. Got you covered. Are you all right?'

Yes, apart from a racing heart and nauseous stomach, and the crippling fear keeping her sprawled on the floor. 'Y-yes.' She tried to clear her throat of some of the dust. 'What about you?'

'Everything seems in working order.'

'What happened? Tell me it wasn't those men in the alley.'

'No idea, but I doubt it.' His hand moved up her leg, reached her knee.

Her hand shook continuously as she reached for Sam's. She needed to feel those fingers gripping hers, to feel his strength and tenderness and warmth. She was frozen. Her teeth chattered. 'Wh-which way is out?'

'Wait there. I'll take a look. Be right back.'

'No.' Her grip tightened around his hand. 'Don't leave me,' she gasped. *Suck it up, Madison. You're a soldier, not a wimp.* It made sense if only one of them did a recon of the situation. Though sense didn't come into it if it meant being on her own, even for a very short time.

An arm wound around her, pulled her against a strong, steady torso. 'You're okay, Maddy. We're okay.'

He was so calm, comforting, at ease. 'Take your time, get your breathing back to normal.' His neck was twisting left then right as he looked around, probably sizing up their position. 'The dust is settling, allowing daylight in. From what I can see, it looks like the roof came down on top of us.'

'That's a lucky break.' The beams might hold the weight of the roof off them. Beams? The fear was back, winding up tighter than ever. 'Fire. There were explosions. There must be fire.'

'Sniff the air, Maddy. I can't smell smoke. Neither can I hear the sound of crackling flames.' His words were measured, calming in their ordinary delivery.

'We don't know for sure.' Fire moved fast, devoured everything in its path. 'The building could be burning further away from us.'

'I'm going to take a look, see how far I can get. Hopefully there's a way out. Wait here. I'll be right back.'

Around the thudding of her heart she implored, 'Sam, be very careful. I don't want anything to happen to you.' She'd go nuts with fear if he didn't return. Suddenly it was impossible to imagine a world without Sam in it.

He cupped her face between both hands and leaned in to touch his nose to hers. 'It won't. I promise.'

'Don't make promises you have no control over.' Then she pushed forward to cover his lips with hers, felt his mouth open under hers, took a quick dip with her tongue to taste him. What if she'd lost him when that explosion blew the bar apart? *You don't have him.* But he was there, under her skin, waking her up, taunting her with possibilities.

His lips returned the kiss, soft and slow and full of something she didn't recognise, not from Sam. It felt like concern and care, almost like love, but she was wrong about that. She didn't know love, had got it badly wrong with her ex. And Sam had clearly told her he didn't get close to people, had indicated he didn't do love.

Sam pulled away, leaving her feeling bereft. 'Don't move,' he told her as he crawled along what used to be a gap between tables and was now full of twisted, broken stools.

Rubbing her hands up and down her arms, she made up her mind to do some exploring of her own, be proactive instead of reactive. Sitting here, waiting for Sam, only led to her mind conjuring up all sorts of nasty ideas about what had happened.

'Looks to me like we're stuck in here,' Sam

told her when she bumped into him under a flat-tened door.

'How stuck?'

'As in the roof is on top of the tables, saving us from being flattened. The walls appear to have fallen inwards. I can't find a way out. Not even a small opening for you to squeeze through.'

No, no, no. They couldn't stay in here, waiting for someone to reach them. She sniffed the air, sneezed when she got a lungful of dust. But no smoke. One bit of luck anyway. A huge bit. 'I'm going to check this out.'

'I'm telling you we're stuck.' He tugged his phone from his pocket. 'I'll text someone on the base.'

Sam was right. She'd known he would be but, desperate for a way out, was driven to check. This was one time she'd love to prove him wrong.

Her hands shook as she felt her way around the edge of their cell. It took less than a minute to concede. Frustration and worry built up inside her, creating waves of nausea. Being confined in a small place would never have bothered her once. 'We could be here for days. No one knows where we are,' she cried.

'They do now.' Sam waved his phone in her direction.

'You're kidding. You got coverage in here?'

'Yep. I've texted Jock and the commander. One of them will get guys here with gear to haul us out.'

She swallowed the fear in the back of her throat. Tried to, any rate. Focused on something else. 'What about the barman? He went to the kitchen. Did you hear anything from him? He might be worse off.' Her heart was in overdrive, beating like that of a wild bird. She couldn't do this. She'd go mad thinking about the last time she'd been stuck, unable to move to save her grandfather.

*There is no smoke. There is no smoke. You're going to be all right. You're with Sam. He won't let anything bad happen to you.*

Both hands were on her stomach, her fingers digging in, warding off any blows that might come her way.

Sam was texting and reaching for her hands

at the same time. 'Stop this, Maddy. You can do better than wind yourself up into a ball of nerves. You're strong.'

Worry was only half of it. But, 'You're right. It's just…' Stop. Don't tell him. He was going tomorrow, and whatever was going on between them would be over. 'This isn't the first time a roof has come down on me. Part of one, any rate.'

Sam stuffed his phone back in his pocket and reached for her other hand. 'Tell me.'

She nibbled her bottom lip until it hurt. 'There was a fire.' Nibble, nibble. 'My granddad lit a candle and set it by his bed.' Her hands gripped Sam's. 'He had early dementia and I was there for the night to give Mum and Dad a much-needed break. The fire investigators believe Granddad knocked the candle over in his sleep.'

Then it became impossible to stop the torrent of words.

'A crashing noise woke me. I rushed to get Granddad out, but there was smoke everywhere and I couldn't find my way around the house I'd lived in most of my life. It freaked me out.'

Sam's hands squeezed hers, his thumbs rubbing her skin softly, encouragingly.

'His room was ablaze. And his bed. I managed to drag him out the door, along the hall to the lounge…'

Her voice trailed away so that her next words were a whisper. She'd never talked about this to anyone. People knew, but putting any of it into words had been beyond her—until today.

'A ceiling beam dropped on us, and that's where we were found not long afterwards.'

Strong arms wound around her. Sam lifted her onto his thighs and held her close, stroking her shoulder. 'We're safe in here, Maddy. There's no smoke or the sound of approaching flames.'

'I've been sniffing the air non-stop,' she admitted against his chest.

'I saw. Now I understand why you freaked out when you saw your first dust whirl.'

'Yeah, that was a bit of a giveaway.'

'But you've done well since. No flinching on patrol where there was dust and smoke for Africa.'

'I work hard at hiding it.' Had to if she wasn't

going to be treated with disdain—by this man and the troops.

'Then there's that stomach rub thing you do when you're upset.' His head might be above hers, but the increased tension in his body told Madison he was waiting for a strong reaction from her.

Damn him for being too observant. She quickly slid off those thighs, muttering, 'Just an old habit,' as she tried to make herself comfortable on the floor beside him, averting her face from his prying eyes in case she let slip some emotions best kept hidden.

'Right.' Sam's disappointment fell between them.

She was damned if she was going to explain so he'd feel happier, because she sure wouldn't.

A phone beeped, and Sam dug into his pocket. Saved by the bell.

'The men are on their way.'

Relief loosened her muscles. 'They know where to come?'

'Everyone knows this place.' He tapped out a text and pushed 'Send'. 'Might as well make ourselves comfortable. They'll be a while putting some gear together and we have no idea what it's like outside our cocoon. They'll have to take it carefully, working through to us. Don't want any more timber coming down.'

'As long as there are no more explosions I can handle that.' *As long as you're with me.* 'Would've loved those koftas, though.'

'I wonder.' Sam tapped his finger against his chin. 'Bix went out to the kitchen to heat up the oil for our order. Then everything blew up.'

'You think the gas might've been leaking? Wouldn't there be fire?' Bang, bang. Her heart rate shot through the roof again.

'No, Maddy. We'd know by now if there was a fire.' Sam leaned back against what was their temporary wall and tugged her against him. 'So, probably not the gas. Guess we're going to have to wait to find out what happened.'

It was warm in the small space, yet snuggling into Sam gave her a different kind of warmth, finally obliterating the chill she'd been fighting since finding herself face down on the floor. He gave her hope they'd be all right. Couldn't ask more of him than that. 'So, got any cards in your pocket?'

He laughed. 'We could try finding a game app on the phone.'

'You'd hate me winning.'

Another laugh. 'Not at all.' Then, 'Okay, maybe a little bit.'

Madison glanced around. For a prison it was quite snug in here. Nothing wrong with the company she was keeping either. 'When I thought we'd spend a day having fun together I never envisaged this.' She'd wanted to make new memories to take into the future as she learned to live without the man she might be falling for, but she'd got more than she'd bargained for.

Seemed her future was going to be all about memories—good and bad. The best she could hope for was the good ones outweighing the bad.

## CHAPTER ELEVEN

'"WE'RE OUTSIDE THE PUB".' Sam read Jock's text out loud. '"Give us a clue where you might be".' In the centre of the café, he tapped back.

'Told you they wouldn't waste any time getting here,' he said to Maddy.

'I'm glad.' There was a quiver in her voice, belying her resolute face.

'It's nearly over, and you'll be back on base before you know it. I'll be able to take a look at that cut on your head then.'

'What cut?' Her fingers tripped around her skull until she found a sticky patch. 'Ouch. Never felt a thing but now it's throbbing.'

'You're relaxing at last.' Stretching his legs out in front of him, Sam tipped his head back against the boards behind them, stared around their tight space. They were incredibly lucky that the roof had fallen onto chairs and tables, creating a safe haven. Three feet either way they'd have been hit and badly injured for sure. Or worse.

He suppressed a shudder, knowing the woman tucked into him would recognise it for the stab of horror it was, and probably freak out a lot more. Maddy had struggled to keep her terror at bay, but it had been there in her eyes, zipping across her face and twisting his gut. He hated that she was frightened, and yet admired her for not going screaming mad. Now that he knew about the fire he marvelled that she was holding it together at all.

It was kind of cosy in here, even if they were trapped. While he should be worrying about getting them out safely, it was the scent that he'd been noticing since Madison's arrival on the Peninsula getting him worked up. Again summer enveloped him. Not any old summer but Christchurch in February when the temperature could be thirty or fifteen in the same hour, where the sky ranged from blue to grey, and the wind had its own agenda. But it was always summer. The trees were green, the farms brown from lack of water, and the locals were at the beach or the parks. Homesickness floored him. 'I've missed home.'

Maddy sat up. 'Lucky for you Burnham's your next posting then. You'll be able to catch up with lots of people in Christchurch, as well as Mr and Mrs Creighton.'

'I suspect I'll be busy. The army has a way of filling our time.' There weren't any others to call on as he hadn't bothered staying in touch much after he'd finished school. *Got Dad's genes there?* Shock blasted him, dried his mouth, curdled his gut. No damned way. But he had walked away from his mates without looking back. What about the guys he'd befriended while training to become a doctor? He knew where most of them were, occasionally emailed to see what they were up to. Not often, and not involved enough to call being friendly.

Maddy's gaze met his. 'Sounds like an excuse to me.'

'That's because it is,' he admitted as he assimilated the truth. He had always walked away from people, had been the one to set the bar. Except for William, who'd become closer than any other friend he'd had, and had been impossible to ignore. Then William had done the leaving.

'How long are you going to stay in the military?' Maddy asked, unaware of his shock.

'I've not decided. It's my career so as long as they'll have me, I guess.' He'd joined to get away from his life, to do something for his country. Now he saw he'd been avoiding the intimacy of a practice in a town with a steady stream of locals and had gone for the broader picture of helping his country and strangers in out-of-the-way places. There'd been no excitement, only a hard slog that had done nothing to make him happy, only sadder that soldiers were even needed in this world. For a while after William died he'd almost had a death wish, had certainly pushed the boundaries when there had been danger in the zone. That was slowly ebbing away. Since Maddy had turned up? Or as a result of too much time away from home, doing as ordered without thought or concern?

She was talking again. Needing to override the sounds of creaking timbers as the soldiers uncovered them. 'You're not interested in getting into surgical practice full-time? It seems a shame when you've done all that training and obviously like the work.'

Glad to be drawn away from where his own thoughts had been headed, he said, 'None of it's wasted, Maddy.' He realised now that the idea of getting into surgery on a full-time basis had been simmering in a corner of his mind. As if he had stopped looking back and was instead now looking ahead for a future to immerse himself in. He instantly put up the usual barriers. 'I'm getting the best of two worlds.'

There had been a time in med school when he'd imagined his own rooms back in Christchurch, a partnership with other specialists to cover a range of medical fields. But the nervous energy that kept him from settling or getting close to people, from creating his own comfort zone, had thrown up the fear he might become bored with being tied to one place and career that would stretch out until he retired many years down the track. Now hauling heavy packs and weapons around a desert no longer held any appeal either.

'I'm hoping to figure out my next moves while

I'm here.' Maddy smiled ruefully. 'Can't see me making the army my life. I'll do all I can as a soldier while here and then I'll make some decisions.'

Did she realise her hands were on his thighs? Heat sizzled from her palms into his upper legs. How was he supposed to ignore her? Turn her away? He was no saint. And right this minute he had to fight with everything he had not to place his hands on her body and feel her, know her, have her. So much so that he daren't even push her hands away as that meant touching her.

Shouts and voices were coming closer, audible over the crashing and banging of timber and who knew what else being moved aside. 'Sam? Madison? Can you hear us?'

'They'll be hearing you back at base,' he called out, relieved at the interruption. Disappointed he wouldn't have the chance to follow through on those heart-stopping sensations Maddy caused him.

'Okay, you two, time you stopped lazing around and got back to camp.' Jock pushed through a gap behind them.

'What took you so long?' Sam growled, despite being grateful for the time he'd had with Maddy. A time of discovery—about Madison and himself. Though he wasn't so grateful for what he'd learned about himself.

'Anyone would think we had nothing better to do than come hauling you out of here.' Jock grinned. 'Next time you're going to town, take a hard hat and an axe.'

Maddy pushed up onto her knees. 'There isn't going to be a next time.'

Somehow that felt like a stab to Sam's heart. As though she was talking to him and not to Jock about where he'd found them.

'Want one of the boys to drive you back to base?' Jock asked.

No, he didn't. 'You heading back?'

'Orders are to look around, see if we can learn what caused the explosion.' Jock eyeballed him. 'Take Madison and fix that bang on her head. Leave this to us.'

Sounded much like an order to him. Sam nodded. 'Sure.' Though he would probably be safer staying here with the troops than spending more time alone with Maddy, he did want to snatch whatever hours he could with her.

'Glad you see things my way.' Jock backed out. 'Follow me, Madison. Keep low or you'll be banging your noggin again.'

The medical unit was empty of all personnel when Madison and Sam pushed through the door. 'Where's everyone?' she asked, looking around. She'd never seen it so empty, so quiet.

'Back in town, cleaning up after us.' Sam dropped his bag of shopping on a desk. 'Let me look at that cut.'

'It'll be fine.' It didn't hurt, though when she had a shower the water would sting a little.

A firm grip on her elbow had her heading towards the treatment room, regardless of any protests she uttered.

'I've gone deaf,' Sam said as he pushed her onto a chair by the bed. 'Now, this might be a little uncomfortable.' His fingers probed her skull, gentle with their touch. 'Not bad. I'll clean it up and put some tape on to keep the dust out.'

Succumbing, Madison sat still and let the fear

and fright of the last few hours wash out of her. Unbelievable that she'd been in another disastrous situation. Unbelievable she'd come out virtually unscathed. 'I wonder what happened to Bix.'

'The guys are searching for him,' Sam muttered. 'Try not to think about him.'

'Easily said.' She drew air into her lungs, breathed in Sam, aftershave and man and sweat. There was comfort in that scent, in the quiet of this room with its walls and roof in their right place, in being safe.

'There.' He snapped off the gloves he'd tugged on moments earlier. His finger lifted her chin so she looked into his eyes. 'You're all good to go.'

'Thank you for being there for me,' she managed around a thick tongue.

'You wouldn't have been there if not because I took you to town.'

'Don't come the guilty party. You didn't blow that café up. It was bad timing, that's all.'

His head was closer to hers now, that mouth so near she only had to lean a bit further upwards and her lips were skimming Sam's.

His hands fell to her shoulders, his fingers splayed and pressing into her.

And all the brakes came off. Not slowly, not one by one, but instantly, freeing her from the restraints she kept wound tight.

She pushed up for a kiss, a deep, bone-melting one that sent shockwaves through her body and aimed for her centre. Heat pooled at her apex as days of withheld desire overwhelmed her. Her hands shoved under his shirt, found his skin, spread across his chest, touched his nipples. It wasn't enough. Tearing at his buttons, she ripped the shirt open and took a nipple between her lips, teased, licked, and ran her teeth lightly across the peak.

Above her Sam groaned. Then he was lifting her, placing her on the bed. Two fast strides and the door was locked. Two strides back and he was lying down beside her, reaching for her.

His erection pressed against her thigh, bringing a moan to her lips. She flipped over, straddled him, felt his sex against her core. Knew she had to have him. Then his hands were under her shirt, gliding over her breasts, satisfying her need to be touched yet rocking her to the core with the intensity of sensations his urgent caresses released.

She was going to make love with Sam. Even as that heat-hazed thought spilled through her mind he was moving his hands downwards, away from her smooth breasts towards her stomach.

'Stop,' she cried, jerking upright.

*No. I can't do it. I won't do it. He'll touch me and that look of horror will fill his eyes. I'd rather have been flattened in the explosion.*

She climbed off his body to sit on the chair with her knees drawn up and her arms wrapped tight around them. 'Sorry,' she muttered. 'I should never have started that.'

Sam was breathing hard as he sat upright and looked at her with nothing but puzzlement in his expression. No censure at all. But he didn't know, hadn't seen. 'Talk to me, Maddy.'

She shook her head. 'No.' What was the point? Been there, and couldn't face a rerun. Especially not with Sam. From the moment she'd seen him across the parade ground the day she'd arrived there'd been some connection between them, and for him to see the scars that distorted her body would destroy that. Even if it was never going anywhere, she couldn't cope with their relationship being reduced to sympathy on his part and agony on hers.

He reached down, took her hands in his, gently lifted her arms away from her knees, opened her to him again. A tremor ran through his body, reaching her through his fingers. She had cut him off in mid-stride when he'd been hard, tight and in need of release.

'That touching your midriff you do? You were injured when that beam came down on you and your grandfather, right?'

Sam's voice was so compelling it coaxed her to look at him, even when she was afraid of what she'd find in his eyes. She gasped. Nothing but care blinked out at her. 'Yes,' she whispered.

'You received burns?' He tightened his grip on her hands as she made to pull free.

Her head dropped downwards in answer to his question. *Now you know, you'll leave me alone. Please.*

'I should've figured that out. It's why you always wear long shirts, isn't it?'

Another nod. 'Are we done?' He didn't need to know anything else.

'Not by a long way. We're only getting started. Look at me, Maddy.'

When she finally did, Sam smiled at her, a long, slow smile that reached his eyes and touched her in places she didn't want touched. Her heart was meant to be unavailable due to fear and vulnerability.

But his smile was continuing the thaw he'd started days ago. She had to stop it before she messed up and let him in. 'No, Sam. I made a mistake kissing you, by taking it further.' He still didn't look upset. 'I am not making love with you. We're not getting close.'

'How long were you in hospital?'

Surprised at his question she answered instantly. 'More than three months while the burns healed and I fought endless infections. Afterwards I took a year convalescing before returning to work at the hospital.'

'That would've put your training behind schedule.'

'It did, but I got there in the end.'

'No side effects?'

She looked away. Her hand covered her tummy where her uterus lay.

Sam's fingers shifted through her short hair. 'Tell me, Maddy. We've come this far you might as well share the whole story.'

She fidgeted with the hem of her shirt. What did it matter if he knew? They weren't going to get together so there wouldn't be any talk of having babies. 'I might be infertile. The worst part of that is I won't know until I try to get pregnant—if I try.' What man was going to accept her on those terms? 'That's the conundrum. Do I ask someone to risk trying with me and watch him walk away when I fail to become pregnant? Or do I accept it's unlikely to happen and work at making my career into something bigger than I'd intended so I won't waste time regretting what I haven't got?'

'That's an agonising decision to have to make.'

Not if she had someone at her side. But she didn't.

'You are amazing, Maddy. So strong to deal with all this.' Sam leaned down for another kiss; a long, slow, burning one.

Maddy fought the incoming waves of need that instantly fired up and began shoving her anguish aside. That anguish was meant to keep her out of trouble. Pulling her head away, she managed, 'Stop.'

He was still holding her hands, and when she tried to withdraw he only tightened his grip. 'Don't.'

'Why? There's nothing to be gained.' Except more hurt.

A sigh escaped Sam. 'I touched your breasts, felt their weight in my hands. For days I've been aware of them pushing out the front of your shirts. They're beautiful, Madison.'

'I got lucky there.'

'Not only there. You're a striking woman who's intelligent, a wonderful doctor, and can sing me into a lather in an instant.' His mouth tipped up into one of those smiles she was coming to recognise as her addiction. Smiles that made her feel special, as though he only gave them to her. 'Don't hide from me. Or anyone. Or life. You're missing out on so much by doing this to yourself.'

'Easy for you to say. Think I should chuck my clothes aside and let a man get an eyeful? See horror or worse fill his gaze just before he turns away from me for ever? I don't think so.'

'Who did that to you?' His arms were cradling her, but he still managed to watch her with fierce intensity.

'Jason,' she whispered.

Of course Sam swore. She'd expect nothing less. While it felt good knowing he was on her side it changed nothing. He asked, 'Is that why your marriage failed?'

'Yes.' So much for the wonderful relationship she'd believed she'd had with her husband if he could leave so effortlessly.

Sam placed the softest of soft kisses on her forehead. Then one on the tip of her nose. 'Don't cry.'

She wasn't aware she was.

Then Sam's mouth covered hers and there was nothing tame about the kiss he gave her. It was deep, intense, and his rising passion told her she hadn't put him off at all. He wanted her.

She wanted him.

Her body arched under his hands as longing pulsed through her veins and moisture pooled at her centre. She wanted Sam.

Could she have him? As in take her clothes off? If she was going to do this then she wasn't going to hide anything. Gulp. Her heart slowed its mad beating. *I can't do it.*

Sam's hands on her shirt-covered waist told her differently. Their tenderness told her she had to, needed to. *Wanted* to.

Her breath hitched in her throat as she began to ease her top up. Her hands shook, her toes curled tight. There was no moisture in her mouth. Get it over with. Drawing in a deep breath, she grabbed the hem of her shirt and tugged it over her head. She didn't want to look at Sam but knew she had to. Words could never tell her the truth as clearly as his eyes would.

In silence Sam regarded her hideous scars, and

no disgust or horror darkened his eyes. Only sadness and acceptance. When his fingers traced some of the marks left by that burning beam she held her breath, unable to comprehend what was happening. He should be running for the hills, or at least saying something condescending. But no. His eyes held only tenderness. Tenderness that changed to awe as he lifted his gaze to her breasts. When his tongue lapped his lips the tension began receding, making her feel light and dizzy.

Sam still wanted her.

Her fingers splayed across his chest. Under one palm his fast heartbeat replicated hers.

Sam wanted her.

With one smooth move Madison stood up to shuck her trousers and panties, tossed her bra to join her shirt. Then she went to work undressing Sam.

'Condom,' he said through clenched teeth.

'You come prepared?' Her heart rate wavered.

'In the top drawer of the desk. For the guys who forget to buy them.'

'How—?'

'Maddy, shut up.' He was kissing her thigh, moving ever upward to where she throbbed with need.

Gripping his head, she held him against her. 'Don't stop, whatever you do.'

His reply was to use his tongue to send shock-waves rolling through her.

She gasped. Her fingers dug harder at his skull. When he did it again she clung to him, not wanting to move for fear of putting air between them.

'I want you,' she croaked. 'I want to touch you, hold you in my hand.'

Slowly he withdrew, lifted her up over his body as he sprawled across the bed. 'You're on top. I want to watch you come.'

Reaching between them, she sought and found his shaft, wound her hand around him. Down, up. He strained against her, pushing up into her hand.

'Let me put the condom on,' he groaned through clenched teeth.

She shook her head. 'That's for me to do.' And she proceeded to, slowly, delighting in the feel of his throbbing manhood. When she couldn't wait any longer she raised herself over him and slowly slid down his length. Sam pressed upward, filling her and still pushing inside. When he withdrew she knew a moment of panic before he filled her again. And again. Pleasure spilled across her lips in a roar, filled the air with acknowledgement of her release.

Sam, oh, Sam. She lay curled, *naked*, in his arms, her head on his still rapidly rising and falling chest. Unafraid of being seen without clothes to cover her scars.

# CHAPTER TWELVE

'DID YOU FIND BIX?' Madison asked Jock the next morning as he packed up his last bits and pieces from the medical unit. Sam was conspicuous by his absence. As he had been since he'd returned to town to help search for the café owner after they'd made love.

'Not in any condition we could take the guy back home.' Jock snapped the latches on his bag. 'Must've taken the full force of the explosion.'

'Was it the gas mains?'

'The verdict is still out and, knowing this place, likely to stay out.' He looked directly at her, said, 'Take care out here, Madison. The dangers aren't always those that you're looking at.'

*Don't I know it?*

If that was commiseration in his face she was going to hit him. She didn't want sympathy for having been an idiot yesterday. She'd take the rap on her chin and get on with soldiering and doctoring. Sleeping with Sam was just another thing to pretend hadn't happened. There was no one to blame bar herself. Sam had given her full warning there'd be no future with him. Knowing those snatched hours would be the end of anything between them before she laid her soul on the line was one thing. *Knowing* it afterwards was…agony. This was knowing with all the emotions she'd promised herself never to suffer again, only now deeper, sharper. Knowing did not soften the blow. She'd fallen for Sam in a bigger way than she'd ever have believed possible. While she wouldn't have to allow for shock and injuries and grief, she wasn't going to wake up tomorrow morning feeling like she had everything under control either.

Jock cleared his throat. 'Madison?'

'Have a safe trip home,' she snapped, and spun away to walk slap bang into the man she'd have sworn had been avoiding her. Of course he had, otherwise he'd have joined her on her run that morning.

'Hey,' he said.

'Hey, yourself,' she retorted, and tried to walk around him.

Sam stepped into her path. 'Maddy, can I have a minute?'

'There's nothing to say, Sam.' He'd kept away from her. Regretting having made love with her? Unable to accept her body after all? Her skin was cold, her heart heavy. She'd known what would happen if she exposed herself and yet she'd gone ahead, thought it was all okay. More fool her. Now she had to move on, go back to protecting herself, and take this as a lesson not to be forgotten.

Desolation stared at her out of those bleak eyes. Desolation that filled her heart, too. 'I think there is.'

'Like what? You're sorry about yesterday? Don't say it, Sam. I don't want to hear you verbalise that.'

'I wasn't going to. I want to explain myself to you.'

'You could've dropped by when you got back last night.' After waiting for him out by the perimeter until late, she'd finally crawled under her sheet to stare into the dark until the sun came up. A fast run first thing had not altered the growing sense of abandonment that had been gathering since he'd headed back to town and left her to face up to having let him in under her guard.

'We were very late. Took some effort finding Bix's body under all the debris.'

'You didn't need to go and help. There were more than enough troops to clear the mess.' Anger vied with sorrow and kept her talking when she really wanted to shut up and see him out of the centre. She was aware of Jock leaving, quietly closing the door behind him, shutting them in together, away from prying eyes. Too late. They were finished yesterday. 'I'll say what I said to Jock. Have a safe trip.'

'Maddy.' Her name was sweet and sad on his lips, pulling at her heartstrings. 'I'm sorry.'

'Sorry because we made love? Or because you can't accept me as I am?'

'No,' he almost shouted. 'Not that. I promise.' He stared at her, shaking his head in disbelief. 'I promise,' he repeated quietly. Was he struggling with that now? He'd denied it but she wouldn't be surprised if he'd found the sight of her daunting despite everything he'd said. She wasn't going to ask. Would rather not know than find out it was true. She'd be crippled.

'Why did you do it if you already knew you were going to walk away? And don't even think of blaming your commitment to non-commitment.' She was trembling. That was solvable if they seriously wanted to have a relationship.

'I could turn that back on you, Maddy. It's not as though I didn't warn you. Why did you have sex with me?'

Sex. Not making love. The coils holding her together that had been slowly unwinding over the past days began tightening again. But she couldn't hold back the truth. 'I couldn't help myself.'

'I wanted you so bad.' Honest, if nothing else.

The anger stepped back, leaving her shaken. 'Once I'd exposed myself I didn't want to hold back,' she whispered.

Sam shook his head. 'But I still shouldn't have gone ahead. I don't deserve you, or the happiness you might bring me.'

'Sugar-coating the situation?'

'Maddy.' His finger was under her chin, lifting her head so she had to look at him. 'Don't go there. I meant it when I said you are beautiful, inside and out. Promise me you won't forget that.'

'Yeah, right.' Somehow his words hurt more than anything else could have. He didn't want a bar of her. She'd read the lack of horror in his eyes, on his face to mean he cared enough to take her as she was. Wrong again, Madison. He'd accepted her enough to have sex, and now he'd had time to think about it he was giving her the heave-ho. Seemed her second attempt at showing a man what had become of her had been little better than the first. At least there were no lies this time. Neither could she deny his warning that he wasn't interested in a relationship, something she might've accepted more easily if she hadn't been expecting his rejection even before they'd become intimate.

Impatient honking from outside the medical unit broke through the tension. Sam's transport had arrived.

'I have to go, Madison.'

Madison, not Maddy. Back to square one. He'd pulled up the barricade. He wasn't just saying he had to get on that truck. She knew it deep down. Had always known Sam would return to New Zealand and she would not feature in the life he made there, or anywhere. She'd known this outcome was coming and had still enjoyed time in his arms, had all but precipitated it. This was the price she'd known all along would come due. But... Did it have to be so hard? Once again everything she wanted, hoped for was being undermined, stolen from her. Because for a few crazed minutes she'd dared to hope. 'Why?' When he said nothing, she asked in a tighter, louder voice, 'You don't even want to stay in touch?'

He looked up at the ceiling, gulped some air, and dropped his head to lock his eyes with hers. Emotion she struggled to recognise had darkened that sky blue to near navy. 'No.'

Ouch. He didn't mince his words. She turned away, unable to look at him any longer as pain saturated her.

'You deserve better. I could take a risk and ask you to join me in life, for life, and I might learn to love you unconditionally. But others I know are missing their chance of happiness because of me. The guilt I carry is too strong to thrust aside. It destroys everything around me. That's all I can say.'

When she turned around he was staring at her as though storing memories, which made no sense when he wanted to leave her, forget her. He should be fighting that guilt, not taking mental pictures of her.

'Goodbye, Sam,' she choked out. She hadn't missed the 'I might learn to love you' bit either. This was the end. The shortest relationship in history. In hers anyway. Until this moment she hadn't realised how much she'd come to care for him. Love him? Absolutely. That's why it was hurting so badly to hear him say what deep down she'd already known.

His finger traced a line from her chin to her mouth, outlined her lips. 'Madison.' Then he turned and walked away.

She watched every step he took across the room to the door, hunger for him gnawing at her. 'Sam, wait.' And she ran to throw her arms around him.

Her heart was breaking as she kissed him, a kiss full of the love she could not tell him about. Then before he could say a word she ran for the office and slammed the door shut.

She would not watch him leave the room. Or climb aboard the waiting truck. In her heart he'd already gone, she didn't need to underline his defection.

She'd get busy going through files and checking stock in the drugs cupboard. She'd quash the anger unfurling in her stomach before it became too big to hold in. Because she was angry—with Sam, but more particularly with herself for letting him close, for falling for him.

Slap. A pile of files hit the desk. Then another, and another. There. Plenty to keep her busy and her mind off anything that wasn't army related. Dropping into the chair, she propped her elbows on the desk and got down to business. She would not acknowledge Sam was gone, wouldn't admit he'd even been here. She'd been a fool to think anything would be different just because she'd laid herself on the line. Now she'd bury the whole episode in work.

But an hour later she raised her head when a plane flew over the base. 'Goodbye, Sam Lowe.'

'That was a boring patrol,' Cassy quipped as she unloaded the medical kit from her backpack in the medical unit.

'Like you want exciting,' Madison retorted. She was more than happy to return to base with no casualties and no bullets fired. 'Or do you?'

'Not if I'm in serious danger,' Cassy admitted. 'Life is for grabbing with both hands, but I might add not if it's at risk of being cut short.'

'I understand.' But did she? The fire had shut her down in every way possible. She'd studied hard to gain her qualifications, and appreciated being able to give back hope to people who were despairing because of a medical condition playing havoc with their lives. But she hadn't moved forward an inch if the heaviness of her heart was an indicator.

Instead she'd repeated her mistakes. Talk about a slow learner. It had to have been hope that had seen her opening up to Sam. It certainly hadn't been common sense. That would've said, *Don't*

*go there because there'll only be one outcome.*
An outcome she was now struggling to cope
with. Despite everything, her dreams were full
of Sam every night. It had been better when she
couldn't sleep, had tossed and turned for hours.

Madison made herself a bitterly strong coffee
in an attempt to crank up her cells and squash
the tiredness dragging her down. She took it out
into the sun.

*Life is for grabbing with both hands.*

Funny how most people didn't get that until
something big threatened or overwhelmed them.
As for her, she'd got it but had determinedly ignored the message, afraid of what waited out
there for her. Her one, brief foray over the line
had bitten back hard. Sam was not, would never
be, a part of her future. He'd made that very
clear.

She'd fought hard to get beyond the results of
the fire, and physically she'd made it. But the
hurt dealt to her heart had remained, had made
her scared to risk opening up to anyone. Then
along came Sam. His reaction to her messed-up

body had been little short of amazing, and she'd been quick to let her desire take over.

But in the harsh light of reality fear still lurked in the shadows of her mind. Because if everything had been fine with him then where was he? Why wasn't she receiving texts and emails from him, telling her what he was up to? Telling her his plans and where he might next be sent with the army?

It seemed he'd been better at covering up his reactions than her ex.

Pulling her knees up, Madison dropped her chin on them and hugged herself tight. Sam had said and done the right things but he didn't want her. Whether that was because of her scars or because he didn't love her, it didn't matter. He didn't want her.

And she'd known it before they'd made love.

Known he didn't love her.

Her own feelings had been hazy until they'd made love.

There'd been sparks between them from the get-go. Sparks. She shuddered. How had she overlooked that? Sparks were dangerous, they burned people with the fire they created. Yet she'd put her heart out there to be consumed.

During the ten days Sam had been gone she'd filled her time and mind with work, and then more work. There were patrols most days, and troops requiring basic medical consults after returning to base. When time was dragging with nothing to distract her she'd go into town to help at the hospital. Most nights she fell into bed without pulling her shirt off, she was that tired. Somehow Sam still raged in her head, never left her in peace.

It didn't seem to matter how hard she tried to banish him, he would not go away. She had let him in because she hadn't been able to keep him out. Extricating him was proving to be beyond her. She needed to get on with finding a different kind of happiness than she'd grown up thinking was her right. It's why she'd come here in the first place, yet in a matter of days she'd lost her way, forgotten everything she'd learned over the past two years. All she had to do now was get back on track, put down plans for the future that wouldn't trip her up.

Sounded absolutely wonderful, if impossible.

Well, what else was she supposed to do?

*Grab life with both hands.*

'Captain, got a minute?' Cassy asked from the doorway.

Her body ached as she unwound from the top step and tipped the revolting coffee into the dirt. 'Sure.'

*Got twenty-four hours' worth of them.*

# CHAPTER THIRTEEN

SAM STEPPED OUT of the Auckland taxi into the drizzle outside the downtown restaurant William's fiancée had recommended for this catch-up.

'Hey, Sam, looking good. The army always agreed with you.' Ally was running towards him from further along the pavement where another taxi was pulling away from the kerb. She leapt at him, threw her arms around his shoulders and plopped a sisterly kiss on his cheek.

Sam struggled to grapple with this welcome after expecting Ally to be quiet and sad. *And* still blaming him. 'Hey, you're looking pretty swish yourself. Being a barrister suits you.'

She slipped out of his arms and smoothed her jacket. 'Isn't that so? It's been a steep learning curve, though.' Now she was quieter, less relaxed with him. More like the Ally he'd been expecting. 'Let's get out of the weather and order some wine. There's a lot to catch up on.'

Oh, he bet there was. Nothing he wanted to talk about but he'd contacted her for a purpose so backing out now wasn't an option. Not if he wanted to start living life to the full again. And he did. If nothing else had come out of his encounter with Maddy it was that he'd discovered how much he'd been missing out on since William's death. Of course that had been deliberate, his punishment. But even jail sentences came to an end, and he sensed his was coming.

Seated in the restaurant's lounge area, wine on the table between them, Sam studied the woman whose life had been tossed upside down by William's death. Where was that crippling sadness that had kept her in bed for weeks afterwards? 'Tell me about the law firm you've joined.' He'd start with the easy stuff, and hopefully Ally would relax again.

Her eyes brightened and her mouth tipped up into a generous smile, though probably not for him. 'I have been so fortunate. All because I studied with the son of one of the partners of

Auckland's top litigation firms. He put my name forward to his dad and before I knew it I had an interview and a job. I'm a very small player in the scheme of things but loving every minute of it.'

'You won't stay on the bottom rung for long, if I know anything about you.' She had a sharp mind and had often talked about the excitement of a courtroom in the middle of a trial.

'I agree.' Her laughter tinkled in the air between them.

Once he'd have given everything to hear her laugh again after William had been taken from her, but now he struggled to understand how she could be so happy. Of course he was pleased for her, but also a little confused. 'I'm glad you've got your mojo back.'

'Oh, Sam, it's so exciting some days I keep thinking I'll wake up and find this job—all of this—was only a dream.' Her smile faded, and the shine of her eyes dimmed.

'So how are you really?' he asked quickly.

'While my career is catapulting me ever upwards, it's not what I'd wished for, planned on.

This is a new life for me, very different from what William and I had been looking forward to.' Ally took a gulp of wine and set her glass carefully on the table.

When she raised her eyes to his Sam felt a frisson of concern slither down his spine. 'I totally understand, and admire you for what you've done.'

'There are days, weeks even, when I'm crippled with missing him.' No need to say his name. They both understood.

'You and me both.' He stared into his glass, then back to her. 'It never leaves me.'

She nodded slowly. 'I wish...' Her sigh was loud between them, filled with all the things she'd once shouted at him—the blame, the anger and pain, the tears.

Sam reached for her hand, covered it with his. 'Don't, Ally. We can't change what happened.' But he'd give his life to do exactly that.

'No, neither of us can,' she whispered through tears.

His heart tore apart for her—again. And for himself. Pain speared him, took his breath away.

He shouldn't have come, shouldn't have called her. But he'd had to, this time for his own sanity. He had to get out of the hole he'd dug himself into, and talking to Ally was the first step. His chest rose. 'I'm sorry, Ally.' When her forlorn eyes met his the anguish and guilt threatened to bury him again. But no. It was time. Time to live Sam Lowe's life, not hover in the dark because of what he'd done to this woman. 'I'll always be sorry for my role in what happened, but I won't say it again. I can't.'

She stared at him, making him squirm, but he didn't back down. He had no idea where this strength had come from but knew it for the truth it was. He'd started living again. The guilt was huge, but it had to be exorcised so he could be free to get close to people he cared about, to love them. But he needed Ally's forgiveness. So help him, he needed that badly.

If it wasn't forthcoming he would be stuck in a holding pattern, going round and round, the army one week, a hospital the next, New Zealand one month, some inhospitable location the next, alone with his thoughts and needs. That was no longer feasible. Maddy had made him start feeling again.

'I'd like another glass of wine.' Ally stood up, empty glass in her shaking hand. 'What about you?'

He had barely touched his. 'Let me get you one.'

A waiter appeared before either of them moved. 'Ma'am? Another?'

With a nod Ally sank back onto her chair, her back rigid, her hands locked together.

What was going on? Yes, he was guilty for William signing on for that fateful tour and thereby destroying this lovely woman's happiness and future, but there was something else in her gaze, her stance. 'Ally?'

'I've booked the table for three people. There's someone I want you to meet. He'll be joining us shortly.'

Sam sank back in his chair. This woman had been all but comatose at William's funeral and for months after. Now she'd found someone else? No, he'd got that wrong. Surely?

'You're shocked.'

'Yes. No.' He dredged up a half-smile. 'I'm not sure what I'm thinking.'

'You're thinking it's too soon, that William's only been gone two years, that I'm not ready. Right?'

'Possibly. But if you're happy then so am I. William wouldn't have wanted you mourning him for ever, missing out on a family, a loving man, a home.'

'You're right. He wasn't a selfish man.' Abby took the wine the waiter placed before her, sipped the liquid, all the while watching him. 'Dave. The guy joining us is Dave, and he's special. We are planning to move in together shortly.'

'I see.'

'No, you don't. You're thinking this is too soon, that I haven't mourned long enough.'

*Am I?* He didn't know. 'How'd you meet?'

'We shared an umbrella one day when it began to rain at the cemetery where we were both putting flowers on our respective partner's graves. Then we had coffee and talked, and slowly over the last few months we've become close.

'I love William, Sam.' Ally's voice was low but

firm. 'I still love him and probably always will in a way.' She swallowed, looked around the room before returning her shaky gaze to him. 'But he's gone and I can't remain unhappy for ever. It's not natural. I want to move on, have those children I'd believed I'd have with a man who's got my back, who will love me always.'

'And has this guy got your back?'

'Yes, Sam, he has. He's quieter and more serious than William, but maybe that's why I fell for him. He's not a rerun. This is a new relationship and I'm not comparing anything.'

Where did this leave him? Guilty as ever? Yep, nothing had changed there. Ally was right: William was gone, couldn't be the father to those children she mentioned or watch her grow old. All because he'd listened to Sam, had been talked into going abroad for another stint in the army.

Now her hand covered his. 'It's okay to start again. It really is. Hanging onto my grief and spending the rest of my life mourning William isn't right.' Her fingers squeezed gently. 'Nor is it for you.'

*You think? But I've left Maddy for that grief*

*and the guilt. I've thrown away the greatest op-
portunity of my life.*

He cleared his throat and tried to speak, but
words failed him.

'Stop blaming yourself. William didn't have
to sign on for that last tour. He'd received his
discharge papers. It was his choice not to sign
them. He had a wild streak, contained by the
army's restrictions, sure, but he liked to get out
amongst it. You didn't force him to do anything
he didn't want to do.'

'He was worried he wouldn't handle settling
down completely.' His pal could be a little crazy
at times. Sam had forgotten that.

'I was wrong to blame you, but I didn't know
how to cope, could hardly open my eyes every
day to face William not coming home to me. It
was so unfair. I had to lash out and you were
the easy target. In the end I realised William
made his own mind up about going, about post-
poning our wedding, about staying in the army,
even though I begged him not to. It's my turn to
apologise for the way I treated you.'

The weight didn't leap off his heart, the bands

holding him together didn't break free, but there
was a loosening deep inside. The start of his future? No, that was too easy. But, 'Thanks.'

'You're not getting off that lightly. Let him go,
Sam. You can't hold onto him any more than I
can. It's not wrong to start living life to the full
again.' Her fingers curled around his hand and
squeezed. 'Please.'

'Now you're rushing me.' This time his grin
was wide and genuine. 'I'm a bloke, remember?
We don't do the emotional stuff easily.'

After an awkward dinner with Ally and her new
man Sam walked along the quay at the edge of
Auckland Harbour, ignoring the drizzle damp-
ening him. His hands filled his pockets, and his
shoulders were hunched as he wandered aim-
lessly towards the Viaduct.

Memories of Maddy fighting her fears
swamped him. She was so vulnerable and yet
tough. She'd told him everything that had happened, had exposed herself to him in a way that
must've taken every drop of courage she could
dig up and then some. But, then, she was strong.

That strength had got her through a devastating time when the man who should've been glued to her side had let her down. The pain of that alone must've devastated her.

Which was why he had to keep away, couldn't change his mind about a relationship with her. He'd hurt her. Somehow, some time, he would let her down.

'It wasn't your fault William died,' Ally had said when she'd kissed him goodbye. 'If he hadn't gone to Afghanistan he'd have found some other dangerous occupation or hobby. It was his nature to push the boundaries way beyond possibility.'

True. So if he wasn't at fault for William's death then what next? Had Ally just freed him to chase life, grab what he wanted and hold on tight?

No, it couldn't be that simple.

Why not? Ally believed he should, he could.

Sam shivered. He might be able to let go of the guilt but getting close to anyone had never been easy. Too many risks.

Water splashed up as he stepped into a puddle. Bring back the desert. A sudden wind brought heavier rain driving at him, chilling him down fast. Time to head for his hotel. He could continue thinking inside the dry warmth with a bourbon in his hand.

The drink warmed him all right, but it didn't solve his dilemma. Madison… Maddy…the woman he'd left behind after she'd given him her heart on a plate. She hadn't voiced the sentiment but that had been love in her eyes when they'd made love. But not when she'd lifted her shirt. No, fear and dread had pulsed out of her then. Had that love given her the courage to open herself up to him? And then he'd walked away because he'd been afraid.

Afraid of hurting her more than she already was. Those scars were harsh, yes, but did they make Maddy less of a sexy, attractive woman? No way. She was still Maddy, the same woman who'd put Porky's foot back together, who'd poured her heart and soul into her singing, who'd become a doctor to help others.

*The woman I've fallen in love with.* Suddenly and abruptly. Frightening, yet exciting, if he accepted the truth.

Was he ready to take the risk? To lay it all out for her to see? What if she left him? There was more than one way to go, and however it happened he'd be devastated, broken.

'Another drink?' the barman interrupted.

'Sure, why not?' He wasn't on duty for the next three weeks. Draining the last centimetre from his glass, he handed it over.

His father had walked away from him and his mother without a backward glance, showing what little importance they'd had in his life. For a wee guy that had been beyond his comprehension. As an adult he still didn't get it, but, then, he'd never seen or spoken to his father since that day so had no knowledge of what had been behind his actions. If his mother had known, she'd never shared it. And then she'd left him, too, when he'd woken up one morning and found her cold in her bed.

'Here you go.' The replenished glass slid into view.

'Cheers.'

Sam glugged down the bourbon. Banged the

empty glass back on the counter and nodded to the barman.

Waiting for his refill, he glanced around the nearly empty bar. Was this what his life had come to? Drinking alone in an impersonal hotel downtown in a large city? Tomorrow he'd fly back to Christchurch and Burnham base, and fill in the weeks waiting for orders for his next move. Except he didn't want to do that any more. Had had enough of moving from camp to barracks to off-the-beaten-track towns.

Maddy had given him a taste of what life could be, a taste of the love he'd craved all his life. He wanted more, wanted it—with her. But most of all he wanted to give love back to her, to show she was cherished, adored by him. To make her feel safe again, to help her find the missing links in her make-up, to love her as she deserved to be loved.

And if something went wrong? If he found himself alone again?

Then he'd have to deal with it. But until then he'd have a life worth having.

# CHAPTER FOURTEEN

CAUTIOUSLY LIFTING HER helmet-protected head above the mound of dirt, Madison scanned the land ahead of her troops. Empty buildings baked in the relentless sun, too far away to hold a threat yet. Between those and the patrol nothing moved. Eventually satisfied they were alone, she called in a low voice, 'All clear.'

Around her soldiers rose to their feet, keeping low as they moved forward, guns at the ready in case their captain was wrong and the sniper who'd attacked a vanload of locals returning to the town after visiting family at a village further away was still out here.

Along with the latest doctor to arrive on base, Madison had spent most of the night in Theatre, putting people back together by sewing up gunshot injuries. She should be exhausted but right now she was revved, running on adrenalin and lots of caffeine. The sniper had to be found and locked up before he hurt anyone else.

'Down,' the leading sergeant called, his hand flicking a signal at them to hit the ground fast. 'Three o'clock, behind the rocks.'

After assessing the layout, Madison led the men out. 'Circle him, and be careful. I do not want to be sewing any of you back together after this.'

'Who needs Captain Lowe when we've got you?' The sergeant grinned.

'Get on with it, Sergeant,' she growled as she swallowed a bitter laugh. *I'm like Sam?* Now, there was a joke. One that would have him in stitches. Sam. What was he up to? Had he managed to wangle another posting overseas yet?

Running low to the ground, she kept beside the sergeant until they reached their target—a filthy, middle-aged man screaming at them in a language she couldn't understand.

Two soldiers caught him, held him still.

'Who have we got?' she demanded of the interpreter.

After five minutes of shouting back and forth

the interpreter informed her, 'He's denying it but I'd say we've got our man. He has no explanation about that gun he was burying.'

Madison shivered. The man must've run out of ammo or he'd have used it on them. 'Call the situation in,' she told their comms technician.

'Just in time,' the private told her minutes later. 'You're wanted back on base.'

'I'm not the only doctor they've got.' Yet she had been acting as if she was, grabbing every case she could, working all hours to fill in the empty days that threatened to knock her down. 'Tell them we're on our way.'

'You enjoy the army, Captain?' her sergeant asked as they bounced and rocked in the truck heading back to base.

'Most of the time.' She was hardly going to say no to someone under her orders. 'Don't like the abrupt way life can go from safe to dangerous in a flash.' Like when that corporal had been hit last week. It had made her wonder if she'd return home in one piece at the end of her stint here, or if there was a bullet with her name on it waiting out in the desert. Thoughts she shoved aside as quickly as they rose. Negative notions were a hindrance to even the sharpest minds and played havoc during the dead of the night.

'Know what you mean,' muttered the sergeant, and that had her wondering what tragedies he'd witnessed. Everyone came with baggage. Everyone.

She knew hers. But she didn't know all Sam's. In the midst of a conversation he'd often gone places she'd been unable to follow. She loved him without restrictions, but there were a lot of gaps in what she knew about him. Making love with Sam had temporarily blown away the last of her barriers. Now he knew everything, had seen everything. But he'd gone without a backward glance, without returning her final kiss. Without showing her the real, deep-down Sam. Had he been protecting her, as he'd said? Or himself?

Madison held the water bottle to her mouth and poured the wonderful icy liquid down her dry, dusty throat as she elbowed the door to the medical unit open. 'Wow, that's good,' she spluttered, and slapped her mouth with the back of her hand.

Cassy followed her in. 'I always drink more when I've been out on patrol. I say it's the dust and heat, but I think fear has a lot to do with it.'

Madison spun around and caught at the nurse's arm. 'Don't let that fear get to you or it'll destroy you.' Hadn't she given herself the same speech on the drive in? And she was going to be fearless from now on? Ha! *Good point, Captain.*

'I know all that, been to the lectures, learned how to cope,' Cassy drawled. 'But...'

'There's always a "but".'

Why were Cassy's eyes widening in confusion? Madison glanced in the direction the nurse was gaping and felt the floor heave up under her feet. Her arms shot out, fumbling for something to hold onto while she retrieved her balance. Finding nothing but air, she tottered forward a step.

'Sam?' He was in Christchurch. Wasn't he? She snapped her eyes shut, flicked them open again. Definitely Sam. 'Ah, hi. We've been on patrol, think the heat got to us.'

He was sitting in her chair, his feet up on her desk, those hands that had done marvellous things to her body behind his head. And, yes, he wore that blasted grin that undid all her good—and not so good—intentions. A steady blue gaze bored into her, so direct, so compelling she could feel her insides melting in an instant what little resistance she'd hurriedly mustered. He was seeing everything she kept hidden. Everything. Surely not? Not that she loved him. She stared back, tightened her spine, tried to hide that L word from her posture, her face, her eyes. *That* he did not need to know.

But something flicked through his eyes. If she hadn't known better she might've thought it was passion. 'Hello, Maddy.' The grin slipped, quickly recovered.

At the sound of that gravelly, deep voice she tipped forward, bending at the waist. So much for standing up to him. Two words and she was lost.

His feet hit the floor and he strode to her, catching her arms and hauling her close. 'I've missed you.'

As her cheek was pressed against his chest, his hand firm in the centre of her back, she drew in his life scent, pure male, full of warnings—and melting the last of her resistance. She'd make a fool of herself if that meant being held by him. Meant being told—

'You missed me?' She jerked back, away from everything she craved. 'Ever heard of email? Your phone gone on the blink?'

Another step back to put more space between them because she couldn't trust herself not to reach for him, to splay her hands over his chest and feel his heartbeat under her palms.

'I prefer using a plane.' The grin had softened into a lopsided smile filled with uncertainty.

'Why?' she asked.

'I need to see you as we communicate, to watch for innuendo and hear the laughter or annoyance in your voice. Email doesn't allow that, and phones can make interpretation difficult.' His eye twitched. 'I only know you well when I'm standing in front of you, reading you as we speak to each other.'

He'd better not have read that L word. 'You've come back to the Sinai to talk to me?' She shook her head in an attempt to clear the dross. 'No one mentioned you being posted back here.'

'I'm on leave. I'm here to see you. Nothing else. I've also taken a discharge from the army, effective next month.'

Her fingers dug into her hips as she tried to remain upright. 'I don't understand.' What did any of this have to do with her? 'The commander knows you're here?'

'He's given me a room in the barracks for the next couple of days, then I'm moving into town to work at the hospital until you're sent home at the end of your tour.'

'I still don't get it. Why would you do that? You hated the desert and heat.'

Sam wanted to chuckle at the stunned expression on Maddy's wonderful face, but he daren't. There was too much at stake. If only she knew how hard it had been not to leap up and grab her to him the moment he'd seen her come into the medical unit. Maddy was not ready for that. She was not ready for him at all. But she was quickly getting over the shock of finding him here, was wrapping herself in confidence, pulling on the feisty armour she was so good at producing. All false, every last piece.

Softness extended through his heart. The woman he loved stood in front of him, holding him at bay with nothing but refusal in her eyes, not ready to trust him. He wanted her ready for everything he had to tell her. Hell, he wanted *her*. So much it debilitated him. That need had driven him to clear the obstacles so he could come to her a free man, but there was a way to go yet. 'I've had a change of heart,' he said, knowing she wouldn't understand. Not until he told her everything and first he needed her to relax. 'I admit to missing home, such as it is. Christchurch is where I grew up, where Ma and Pa Creighton are. Where you'll return to at the end of your time in the army. I want to be there when you do.' Maddy wasn't usually slow on the uptake, but he wondered if she'd realise he'd wound her and home into the same package, that he needed both to become one for him to make her happy.

'Sam.' Her fingers were white as they dug deeper into her flesh. 'It's great to see you but I'll have to catch up later. I'm needed elsewhere.'

'If you're referring to the message sent through comms, that was from me. I had them send it.'

'You couldn't just wait for me to get back?'

'I hate thinking of you out on patrol, looking for snipers. It was my way of saying come back safe.' It was true. From the moment he'd walked in here and learned Maddy was with a group hunting out a sniper, he'd been gripped with fear. So much so that when she'd walked in as though back from a stroll to the shops he'd alternately wanted to kiss her and shout at her.

'It's the job, Sam.' The bite had gone from her voice.

'Yeah.' He glanced around, only now aware of everyone watching them. 'Let's go somewhere private.'

'On an army base?' Her eyebrow lifted in a cute fashion, sending ripples of longing through him. 'You haven't been gone that long to forget what it's like.'

The office had been very private the afternoon they'd made love. 'Want to walk the perimeter?'

'I'm done with the sun for today.' She whistled

silently. 'We could grab a water and find a corner no one else is interested in.'

At least she hadn't kicked him into touch. 'Let's.'

'Where will you live when you're working in town?' Maddy asked as they settled on outdoor chairs in a private spot behind the barracks block.

'There's a small hotel on the same street.'

The plastic bottle spun back and forth in her hands. Her eyes seemed to be focused on a lone blade of grass at her feet. Then her head came up and she said, 'Okay, what's this about?'

Should he leap in? Or lead up to the crux of his visit? He leapt. 'You and me. I love you, Maddy. That week we worked here together pulled me up short, brought me to my knees.'

If he'd expected her to leap into his arms he was out of luck. Her widening eyes were the only indication that she'd heard him. 'Yet you went away without telling me. What's changed?'

'Me.'

Maddy stared at him, her lips parted and her eyes wide. 'Go on.' She wasn't making it easy for him but, then, she had a lot at stake. She wouldn't be wanting to risk having her heart smashed again.

If she loved him. Cold fear slid over him. What if she didn't? She wouldn't have made love that day if she didn't, surely? Not Maddy. Not with her insecurities.

'I know I told you I'd never let you close, that my heart wasn't available. I did that because I was afraid. I've fought becoming too close to anyone because I couldn't face being left again.' He'd told her that before, but needed to remind her before going on. 'When William was killed in Afghanistan I blamed myself for talking him into going with me. I believed I didn't deserve love and happiness.'

'And now?'

'We each are responsible for our choices in life. William could've stayed home and got married, as was planned.'

Maddy nodded abruptly. 'Go on.'

She was tough. 'That first day I saw you walking across the parade ground? That's when I fell for you.' Just hadn't recognised the emotions rolling through him at the time.

She swallowed hard, but remained silent.

'I've never stopped loving you from then on, Madison.'

She leapt to her feet, stormed over to the fence and stared out across the sand. Her hands were gripping her hips, her legs spread wide.

He waited, and waited. The next move was hers.

His water was gone by the time she turned and walked back to him. His heart rate was off the scale.

'Is this when you head away again?' she asked in a strangled tone. Then she began shaking, her hands, her legs and shoulders, her teeth chattering.

'No. Never.' Sam leapt up, pulled her into his arms. That soft body was home for his starved one, warming him where he'd been cold for years. Her scent his beacon. 'I want to marry you, have you at my side for ever.'

She jerked and his arms were empty. 'No,' she cried.

'Maddy.' Another chill overrode the warmth. 'Is that so bad?'

She spun away, spun back to stare at him. Tears poured down her cheeks. 'You love me?'

'With all my heart.'

She slumped, pain removing all the colour from her cheeks. Her hands gripped her midriff. 'Have you thought this through?' she gasped through those tears he desperately wanted to wipe away. 'Considered everything? Like possibly never having a family?'

'Maddy, it's you I want, I love. If we have children I'll love them, too, but if we find we can't then I won't stop loving you because of it.'

Longing warred with denial in her face. 'You're talking for ever here. Have you really thought what that means? I couldn't cope if you changed your mind.' Her breasts rose on a breath. 'Go back to wherever you've decided is home, Sam.' Her tears had become a torrent, and she stumbled as she started to run—away from him.

'No way, Maddy. No damned way. You and I belong together.' He caught her up in his arms, lifted her feet off the ground, held her against his body.

She writhed and wriggled, trying to get away from him. Her sniffs were muffled against his shirt.

'I love you, Maddy. I love you. As in now. I always will. I love you, Maddy.' Over and over the words spilled between them. 'I love you.' His hands soothed, his body sheltered her from herself, and slowly, oh, so slowly, she calmed. He eased his embrace enough to let her stand against him, but he did not drop his arms from his woman.

Finally a shudder rippled through her length and she pulled back to rub her arm across her swollen face. Then she looked up at him. Hope swam in those wet eyes. And something else.

Sam held his breath.

Finally she spoke so quietly he had to lower his head to hear her. 'I love you, too, Sam.'

All the air in his lungs rushed across his lips. *She loves me.* That was all he needed. All he'd ever wanted. Pulling her back into his arms, Sam kissed those swollen lips.

When he stopped to draw breath she told him, 'There must've been something in the air the day I arrived here. Not only dust. I think I started to feel hope for the future when you didn't laugh at my meltdown. I'm ready now, ready for whatever we might face. With you beside me I can cope with anything.'

Putting his finger on her lips, he managed, 'Shh…'

As he leaned close to reclaim those lips his own tears splashed on her face. She tasted of love and hunger and the future. And of a home together, a life together.

She was his life.

# EPILOGUE

*Five months later...*

MADISON TAPPED HER foot impatiently as the Christchurch immigration officer studied her arrivals card. All around her people seemed free to go, while she was stuck with this annoying man.

'Whereabouts in the Middle East have you been?'

'The Sinai Peninsula. With the army,' she added for good measure, hoping that'd hurry him along.

'I see you're not with your contingent today.'

'They're coming next week. I'm getting married in seven days and was given an earlier flight.' One with seats and food and cabin crew. Yahoo.

Tick, tick. He finally smiled. 'There you go, Captain. Have a great wedding.'

'Oh, I intend to.' Her pack bounced on her back

as she ran for the exit and charged out into the wide space. 'Sam,' she shrieked. 'Sam.'

'Over here.' And there he was. That smile she'd been craving since he'd headed home to finalise details for their wedding and to pick up the deeds to the house they'd bought last month on the net after her family had checked it out for them.

'Sam.' She dropped the pack and leapt at him, wrapped her arms and legs around him tight. She was never going to let go of him again.

He staggered but didn't drop her. 'Maddy, babe, what took you so long? I've been waiting twenty minutes.' That smile widened into a grin, and his hands splayed across her waist, firm, warm and demanding. 'I've missed you every second of every day.'

'I've missed you more,' she teased, before plastering her lips back on his, and forgetting everything but the man holding her. Her fiancé, the man she'd fallen in love with as quickly as a lightning flash could cut through the sky. Finally she removed her mouth enough to whisper, 'Take me home'. To the house they were going to have so much fun making into a home. Their home.

They weren't having a decadent honeymoon on an island beach in the Pacific or at a swanky hotel in Australia. Nope, they were staying at home, buying furniture and linen and kitchen utensils, and all the things necessary and not so necessary to fill their home and make it comfortable. And finding rooms to set up their joint surgical practice in.

Sam held her away from him to lock those gorgeous blue eyes on her. 'Hate to spoil the fun but we are not alone.'

'Really? Who's here?' She stared over his shoulder and right into the amused gaze that she'd known all her life. 'Dad.' She leapt from Sam to her father, wrapping her arms around him. 'I've missed you.'

'And me you, sweetheart. Glad you're back safe and sound.'

Then she was being swarmed by the rest of her family, and the tears streamed down her face. Who would've believed six months ago she'd be coming home to all this? 'Sam?'

'Right here, Maddy.' He leaned close and whispered, 'It's all real, right down to that chocolate stain on little Midge's brand-new shirt she wore specially for Auntie Madison.'

'And how did she come by chocolate?' Her sister wouldn't have let Midge have it.

'Seems there was a lot of it hanging around on the shelves in the book store over there and, well, we just couldn't walk past without helping the shopkeeper out by buying some.' Sam was grinning down at her nieces.

Maddy's heart swelled. That grin had a lot to answer for. It had snagged her right from the get-go, and still made it hard for her to ignore Sam. But now it had changed. There was no hidden agenda behind Sam's grin, no challenge, nothing to suggest anything other than he was happy.

Stretching onto her toes, Madison kissed her man. 'I love you so much it's scary.'

'I know what you mean but let's not be afraid. We've got too much good going on to be side-tracked by what might be out there waiting for us.' With another kiss he set her on her feet again. 'There are two people here who are busting to meet you.'

Of course. She should've gone to them immediately. 'Ma and Pa Creighton. I am thrilled to finally meet you.' It was easy to hug this woman who'd been so kind to Sam and his mother, easy to accept a return hug.

'It's us who are thrilled.' Ma Creighton stepped back to swipe at her cheeks where small tears tracked a line through her make-up. 'Sam's so happy. We've never seen him like this. Thank you.'

'Don't thank me. We're in love. That tends to make even grey days look sunny.'

'What my wife isn't saying is that you've brought Sam home to us. As in he drops by all the time, has meals with us, talks as though he's got to make up for all the years we've known him.'

'I'm glad. Really glad. He adores you both.'

'Right.' Sam started rounding everyone up. 'Time we headed home.' He was looking at Maddy and when he said 'home' his eyes lit up with excitement. 'Maddy hasn't seen her house yet and I can't wait any longer to show her.'

There was a general groan from everyone. 'Guess that means we should take our time getting there.' Maggie laughed.

Definitely, thought Madison.

'Definitely,' muttered Sam. 'Take about three days.'

Madison skidded to a halt in front of the terminal doors now sliding open. 'We haven't got a chance of being alone until this lot have had dinner.'

'I figured.'

She grabbed his hand. 'Come on. I need you to myself for five minutes.'

'A quickie on the way home?' Sam wiggled one eyebrow at her.

Her elbow jabbed him in the side. 'I have a present for you.'

'What is it?'

'Patience, man. Where's our car? What colour is it?'

'Aren't you supposed to ask what make it is first?'

She kissed the back of his hand that held hers. 'How many seats has it got?'

'Four.' He dragged out his answer, confusion darkening his eyes.

'Has it got a large boot?'

'Ye-es. Maddy…?'

'It's just that we're going to need all of that. There's going to be a third member of this family arriving in seven months' time.'

'Maddy!' Sam said as he dropped her bag and swung her up into his arms. 'Seriously? We're going to be parents?'

A tidal wave of happiness rolled through her and she clung to the man who had helped her get her life back on track. 'I love you, Sam Lowe. Always will. And, yes, we're going to have a baby!'

* * * * *

*If you enjoyed this story,*
*check out these other great reads*
*from Sue MacKay*

*THE ARMY DOC'S BABY BOMBSHELL*
*DR WHITE'S BABY WISH*
*BREAKING ALL THEIR RULES*
*A DECEMBER TO REMEMBER*

*All available now!*

# MILLS & BOON®
## Large Print Medical

## October

| | |
|---|---|
| **Their One Night Baby** | Carol Marinelli |
| **Forbidden to the Playboy Surgeon** | Fiona Lowe |
| **A Mother to Make a Family** | Emily Forbes |
| **The Nurse's Baby Secret** | Janice Lynn |
| **The Boss Who Stole Her Heart** | Jennifer Taylor |
| **Reunited by Their Pregnancy Surprise** | Louisa Heaton |

## November

| | |
|---|---|
| **Mummy, Nurse...Duchess?** | Kate Hardy |
| **Falling for the Foster Mum** | Karin Baine |
| **The Doctor and the Princess** | Scarlet Wilson |
| **Miracle for the Neurosurgeon** | Lynne Marshall |
| **English Rose for the Sicilian Doc** | Annie Claydon |
| **Engaged to the Doctor Sheikh** | Meredith Webber |

## December

| | |
|---|---|
| **Healing the Sheikh's Heart** | Annie O'Neil |
| **A Life-Saving Reunion** | Alison Roberts |
| **The Surgeon's Cinderella** | Susan Carlisle |
| **Saved by Doctor Dreamy** | Dianne Drake |
| **Pregnant with the Boss's Baby** | Sue MacKay |
| **Reunited with His Runaway Doc** | Lucy Clark |

# MILLS & BOON®
## Large Print Medical

## January

| | |
|---|---|
| The Surrogate's Unexpected Miracle | Alison Roberts |
| Convenient Marriage, Surprise Twins | Amy Ruttan |
| The Doctor's Secret Son | Janice Lynn |
| Reforming the Playboy | Karin Baine |
| Their Double Baby Gift | Louisa Heaton |
| Saving Baby Amy | Annie Claydon |

## February

| | |
|---|---|
| Tempted by the Bridesmaid | Annie O'Neil |
| Claiming His Pregnant Princess | Annie O'Neil |
| A Miracle for the Baby Doctor | Meredith Webber |
| Stolen Kisses with Her Boss | Susan Carlisle |
| Encounter with a Commanding Officer | Charlotte Hawkes |
| Rebel Doc on Her Doorstep | Lucy Ryder |

## March

| | |
|---|---|
| The Doctor's Forbidden Temptation | Tina Beckett |
| From Passion to Pregnancy | Tina Beckett |
| The Midwife's Longed-For Baby | Caroline Anderson |
| One Night That Changed Her Life | Emily Forbes |
| The Prince's Cinderella Bride | Amalie Berlin |
| Bride for the Single Dad | Jennifer Taylor |